THE DRAGON

A NOVEL BY

ZARA DAVIS

Title: The Dragon

Author: Zara Davis

Printed in the USA

Kingston Imperial
info@kingstonimperial.com

First Edition:

Book and Jacket Design: Laura Dapito

Cataloging in Publication data is on file with the Library of Congress

Paperback: ISBN: 9781954220768

eBook: ISBN: 9781954220775

A NOVEL BY

ZARA DAVIS

Six years later, it still hurt like hell.

He would have given anything to swap places with Maria because she should have been here for all of this daily, and doing it alone was killing him. No one deserved the joy of their little girl more than his wife did. They'd laid awake at night talking about everything they dreamed for Ryu. Sometimes, she'd sleep on the nursery floor while he painted the ceiling with stars and would make wishes on the shooting stars as he colored them in. Some of those dreams were the same ones he'd repeated when the machines kept her alive. All she'd ever wanted was to be a mom.

For her to come so close but never actually experience that moment, holding her little girl in her arms, was nothing short of tragic.

They'd written their own vows. He'd spent weeks working on his and, in the end, had settled upon a few straightforward words where he called them wolves because wolves mate for life. When he'd made that comparison, he'd meant it. There would never be another woman for him. There hadn't been a minute in a single hour of any day in those six years since he'd considered bringing anyone else into their lives.

It was him and his little girl against the world.

They were a team.

Hers was all the love he needed.

Smiling, he watched his little girl and her best friend come running towards the car. He might have seen the man in the mirror if he hadn't been watching them. He had his hands shoved into his pockets and his head down and was walking without really picking his feet up—more of a shuffle than a stride—but with urgency, covering the sidewalk fast. He didn't look as he crossed the road, coming up level with the driver's window.

There is no sound in the world like a gunshot. It is instantly recognizable, ringing out on a primal level to which the animal within us all responds. That single shot tore through the quiet street. Everyone froze mid-thought, mid-step; instinct took over, and they scattered, running for cover. Everyone excellent Ryu, who stared at her father's blood sprayed across the glass of the passenger window. She kept on walking until she was close enough to reach out and touch the glass, unable to look away from the dead eyes of her father. She couldn't break eye contact, no matter how desperately she wanted to look away.

Her entire world was gone. Snatched away by a single gunshot.

The street filled with screams. Panic. Dread. Children came racing down the dance school's steps. Frightened parents rushed across the concrete yard, scooping them up and carrying them out of sight of the shooter.

Still, Ryu couldn't move.

The man with the gun knelt beside her, close enough for her to taste the foulness of his breath as he leaned in to whisper, "I would have killed you, too… but he needs you to live for now. So run, girl. Run."

At that moment, amidst the screams and the whirling chaos, the street awash in a tapestry of terror and confusion, Ryu found herself alone, her world shattered into a million pieces, and she felt the weight of her name like never before. She was a warrior. A dragon. And dragons did not cower. They roared.

CHICAGO: NOVEMBER 1ST 2022

ONE

She was a system kid, bounced around from home to home, unwanted most of the time, disliked some of the time, and abused more often than was right, but Ryu was a survivor. One foster father had used cigarettes to burn the soles of her feet, and another had demanded she blow him. She took the pain and ran away from other degradations. There had been good families, too, but she never seemed to stay there long before Family Services moved her along.

She wasn't easy. She knew that. She was damaged. How could she not be? Ten years was a lifetime in some regards, but when it came to that freezer-burned memory of her father's face resting up against the glass with the blood running down it or the stranger's whispered order demanding she run, that was all so fresh it might have happened yesterday. And it hurt every bit as much as if it had.

The only constant in her life was Indigo. She'd been beside her that day and every day since. Indigo was more than just her best friend. They were sisters in every way but blood. And one thing about Indigo was that she took no shit; it didn't matter who from, either. It was a blanket. No fucks given, no shit taken credo. Ryu had a small coterie of friends. She didn't need them. Not when she had Indigo. It was about the quality of friends, not the number of them. They weren't Pokemon.

The girls sat on the wall, watching younger kids popping and locking as a tinny cellphone pumped out beats, goading each other into more elaborate moves; top rocks, down rocks, power moves, and freeze. Whooping and hollering filled the street, drowning out the sound of sirens a couple of blocks over. She didn't dance anymore. She hadn't since that day. But that didn't mean she didn't like watching others.

A couple of corner boys traded dime bags with people who wouldn't have crossed the street to piss on them if they were on fire ordinarily, but they wanted to party, and the boys had what they needed to make their night uninhibited.

A block over, she heard a sound that made her blood run cold. A siren. It was a Pavlovian response, her subconscious associating the sound of sirens with the cops and paramedics who had taken her father away from her.

She hopped down from the wall, not wanting to be there, when the cop car turned into the street.

"C'mon," she told Indigo and started running.

Running.

If any single word could ever be said to sum up a teenager's life, it was that one for Ryu. Running. Ever since her father's murderer had whispered, "So run, girl. Run," into her ear, she hadn't stopped.

She darted across the road and disappeared down an alley between two tenements, coming out on a back alley that ran almost a mile between yards filled with scrap, bedsteads, broken furniture, cords of wood, and other junk. An old boy sat on a stoop, smoking a licorice paper cigarette, while his woman hung out the washing on the line, balancing a baby on her hip. Better yards were scattered throughout the junkyards, with grass; a few even had trees and shacks used as workshops. He waved at the girls as they walked down the path.

Coming out the bottom of the path, Ryu saw an expensive Ford Taurus with tinted windows parked up against the curb, engine idling. It was the kind of car you didn't look twice at because you didn't want whoever was behind the wheel taking an interest in you. Best case, it had municipal plates and a couple of antenna, meaning it was an undercover cop car, worst case, it was a crew car, the tinted glass meant to deter prying eyes. Of course, the bangers preferred tricked-out cars, so it was more likely to be undercover cops.

She didn't look as she bolted across the road and didn't turn around at the sound of the Taurus's engine starting up.

Indigo could barely keep up with her, even with a lifetime of practice chasing after her best friend.

Two more streets, two more alleyways, and they emerged across the road from Ryu's latest home. It was one of the good ones. She could see Eileen through the window, busy making dinner. Stepping through the front door, the first thing she smelled was the brisket, and it was heavenly. She was playing Aretha and singing as she cooked. Eileen had a good voice. Soulful. The fragrances and the songs made the house feel like a home. Ryu bustled in, calling, "Is it okay if Indy stays for dinner?" knowing she wasn't giving her foster mom much choice, but it didn't matter because Indigo stayed for food most nights.

The girls laid the table in the front room and then rushed up to her bedroom, where they leaped onto the twin beds and put the music on. The room was a typical teenager's room, with posters on the walls. Still, when you looked closer, you might have noticed the slightly schizophrenic nature of the bands adorning them, with some being particularly childish choices compared to the more grown-up taste of Ryu. That was because she shared the room with her twelve-year-old foster sister, Talia.

Some kids looked like butter wouldn't melt in their mouths, but the reality was anything but sweetness. Talia was one of those. But she was twelve, and she wouldn't be told. She didn't care if her choices were wrong because she had a lot of life left to put them right. She only cared about having fun, even if that meant running with devils rather than angels.

She was hardly ever home, regardless of curfew, and it didn't matter how often Ryu warned her there were worse places out there; the girl was determined to push Eileen and Jack, running their patience out, and ended up being sent away.

Ryu had no idea where the girl was now, probably hanging around with the corner boys, on the hook as they swaggered and preened, strutting and making out like they were really something, and she was just too young and too dumb to see through it. Give it a couple of years, and she'd be more worldly. The problem was how deep she would be before she realized she was swimming with sharks.

The girls spent more than an hour talking about nothing with all the breathless enthusiasm only girls of a certain age could muster, about nothing much at all.

They heard Jack coming home, then the call to dinner a little while later.

Talia was away. Eileen didn't make a big thing out of it, but it is evident that Jack wasn't happy. Ryu offered to go find her and drag her ass back home, but her fosters just shook their heads, "Let's enjoy while it's hot, shall we? She can have leftovers."

"Assuming there's any left," Indigo said, licking her lips and rubbing her hands together like she'd just stumbled upon the motherlode.

Jack laughed and started carving while they each helped themselves to vegetables, then passed their plates around for him to lay the cuts on.

Conversation while they mainly ate revolved around what he'd done at work and what they'd done at school that day. Safe subjects. Right up until Jack asked, "Any of you notice the car hanging around outside? Looks like cops trying to hide and sticking out like a sore thumb?"

"I saw them," Ryu said, "but they were a few streets over."

Eileen went over to the window and pulled the net curtain a few inches back to peer out. "Well, now they're parked up across the street."

"Is there something I need to know?" Jack asked the girls.

Both of them shook their heads. Ryu mimed 'cross my heart' to back up her denial. "That doesn't mean they're not looking for Talia, though," she said.

"Let's try not to jump to conclusions," Eileen said, letting the curtain fall back into place. "So, what have you girls got planned for the evening?"

"Got a hot and heavy date with Netflix," Ryu told them, earning a snicker from Indigo.

"Sounds like fun," Jack said. "Want me to rustle up some desert?"

"It's all good, Mister C.," Indigo assured him. The C stood for Calveccio. Irish Italian. Jack worked in a bakery as a pastry chef. His deserts were works of art.

"If you're sure? It's no trouble."

"We've got pudding cups; we're fine," Indigo said, enjoying the way he screwed his face up as though the idea of store-bought pudding cups was a personal affront. She grinned, earning a shake of the head from Ryu.

The girls disappeared upstairs to watch TV, leaving the grown-ups to do the dishes and worry about the car across the road and the men inside it, watching their house.

TWO

It was quiet.

Shadows played across the wall like one of those ancient puppet theaters. Skeletal branches became swords and clubs that beat the shadow monsters to death. Ryu couldn't sleep. Indigo was flat and snoring on the floor, with most of her sleeping bag kicking off around her knees. Most of her hair was a tangled knot across the front of her face, blowing up from her lips with each exhalation.

Her fosters were asleep in their room down the hall.

Talia still had yet to come home.

When she heard the door downstairs, she assumed it was her wayward sister coming home, probably drunk or high, but she didn't hear a single set of footsteps coming up the stairs. She heard more. At least two. And they sounded heavy. Something prickled at the nape of her neck. Ryo rolled out of bed, grabbed a couple of her pillows, and padded up the comforter so it looked like someone was huddled under it; then, with a hand over Indigo's mouth, she woke her, shaking her head to keep her friend from calling out, and whispered, "*Someone's in the house.*"

Indigo's eyes flared wide, panicked, but she battled it down, nodded, and slipped out of the rest of her sleeping bag. She was in a fleecy red and white check pjay's and a candy-colored tee that barely covered her midriff. Ryo wore fleecy shorts and a heavy fleece overshirt that was far too oversized for her. Both were barefooted.

She heard movement outside her room.

Saw shadows move beneath the doorway.

Then, heard Jack challenge the intruders. "Get the fuck out of my house unless you want to—" he never got to finish the rest of the sentence; his words were cut off by the staccato rattle of gunfire ripping through the dark night. The next sound Ryo heard, in the deafening silence that followed, was her foster father's body hitting the floor.

Her phone started vibrating on the nightstand. Eileen's name was on the display. She snatched it up so that the rattle and hum couldn't give her away, in time to hear her foster mom swallowing down tears and horror to say the one word she hated more than any other, "Run!" She didn't argue. She gestured for Indigo to open the window in her little en-suite bathroom that led out onto a fire escape. "Find your little sister. Keep her safe. I'm trusting you, Ryo. Keep her safe. Please."

"I promise," she whispered, barely daring to breathe.

"I know you will. Now go, girl. Run. And don't stop running until you find Father RA. He will know how to help you… I wish we could have done more for—" A second burst of gunfire ripped through the house. There were no screams. No taunts from the attackers. Nothing to say why they had come in the night, why they had killed Jack and Eileen. It didn't make sense. But she couldn't stand there, shaking her head in denial like an idiot. That way, she ended up every bit as dead as her foster parents. Thinking fast, she grabbed her bed and dragged it across the door, knowing that no simple pillow subterfuge would buy her the time she needed to get out of there, and rushed into the bathroom behind Indigo.

Her best friend was already halfway down the fire escape.

Ryo didn't have time to think.

She saw the car down there—the same one that had been watching the house earlier, with its lights on, picking out the alleyway where the fire escape emptied out.

They battered at the door behind her.

It would keep them out of the room for a couple of seconds.

If she followed Indigo down, she'd bring them with her, like it or not, meaning there was every chance she'd be killing her best friend. So, she did the only thing she could. She went up, and she hoped the killers followed her.

THREE

The iron clanged beneath her, louder than anything her bare feet could have been responsible for. Heavy boots. Military style. She glanced down and saw two men, both in paramilitary fatigues, black, with AK47s pointing up at her. Their faces were blacked up, so the only thing she could see with any clarity, lit up by the streetlights, was the whites of their eyes.

With a quick 'follow' gesture, the first man started up after her.

The brownstone wasn't that high; four stories, with a sloping roof, clay tiles, and chimneys. There was a five-foot gap between it and the neighbor and another five-foot gap on the other side. But three doors down, those gaps widened to make way for an alleyway between the buildings. That one, she realized, even as she cut off her options, was more like ten feet across, but the next house was only three stories. She didn't have a choice now that she was committed to this course.

Ryu realized she'd grossly miscalculated long before she launched herself off the edge of the third building.

Because it wasn't ten feet.

It wasn't even close.

But she was as quick with her mind as she was with her feet, and even as she found herself kicking out over the dizzying drop between the first and second houses, she was taking in her options, looking for alternatives, and making a choice that, if she got it wrong, would end up with her pancaked on the blacktop below. The flat roof was an obstacle course of washing lines, a few with stray bits of clothing still pegged to them but others hanging slackly. She stuffed her phone in the back pocket of her plays and fumbled with the ties on one, unraveling it from the post and wrapping it around her wrist, then used it as a tether as she swung out over the wider gap. As the world fell away beneath her, she hung in the air, then started walking down the wall, playing out the nylon line until it snapped tight, biting into her wrist. She was still ten feet from the ground, which was a long way to deliberately fall.

But she had no choice.

Clinging onto the line with her free hand, Ryu unwrapped her wrist and, with nothing to hold her, fell.

The phone fell faster, shattering on impact.

She hit the ground hard a second after it, half-stumbled, half-rolled forward, coming down onto her shoulder and grazing her hands and knees. She gasped and saw the first face peer down over the roof's edge, scrambling out of the line of sight. Back pressed up against the wall, she listened.

Running.

The slap of bare feet on the blacktop.

Indigo.

Ryu stepped out of the shadows, scaring the life out of her friend, whose scream betrayed their position; even before Ryu could cut it short with a hand over the mouth, grabbed Indigo's hand and dragged her between more houses, back onto the same cut that ran between the streets that they'd walked down earlier.

But this time, they had somewhere else entirely in mind for a destination.

She heard the rumble of the car engine a street over and

knew the killers were trying to follow them, even if they were going where cars couldn't follow. Pain lanced from her feet, but she couldn't think about it. She needed to run, even if it left her feet a bloody mess. The alternative was the killers catching up with them. And she couldn't think about that.

Head down, gritting her teeth, Ryu ran, arms and legs pumping furiously, sweat streaming down her back until her thighs burned, and a searing pain sliced through her side, and she ran some more.

Indigo chased her, not understanding what was going on.

With the car's engine haunting every corner and possible avenue of exit, Ryu kept running through the burning lungs and blazing muscles, looking for a way out they would never expect. But with the hunters following her and the avenue seeming to go on and on, she was out of options unless she used her head and turned things around. It was tempting to return the way they'd come; the hunters in the car wouldn't expect that, but what if the men they'd left behind were still there and they walked right into their guns?

"This way," she said, seeing a light in a back window. She was over the fence and dropped down into the backyard silently. They were looking for her on the ground now, so where better to go than up? Creeping through the backyard, she needed Indigo to boost her up so she could clamber onto the sloping roof of a lean-to-outbuilding and scramble up the rusted iron ladder of the fire escape to the roof. It took a few minutes and made more noise than she liked. Still, soon enough, both girls were lying pressed flat against the tarpaper, looking up at the night's thousand eyes, breathing hard, and trying to think through what had to happen next if they weren't going to end up as dead as Ryu's foster family.

"Who were they, Ryu?"

She shook her head, but her friend couldn't see her.

She didn't have an answer anyway.

She was numb.

The grief would hit her later. But for now, there were other things she had to worry about, like Talia, her foster sister, because there was nothing to say she was safe. If the men in black had wanted to wipe them all out, then Talia was a loose end, meaning she was in danger, wherever the hell she was. And Ryu doubted that her new 'friends' in that crew of hers would risk their own skin trying to help her. So, it was down to her. Again. Like it always was.

But it felt different this time because she was doing it for Eileen, the same way Eileen had looked out for her every day since she'd turned up at their door.

She felt the sting of tears on her cheeks but didn't wipe them away.

"Talia," she said, so softly Indigo thought she'd imagined it.

When she realized what her friend meant with that one word, she said the only thing she possibly could, "Oh shit. We've got to get to her. You know who she's running with?"

"Yeah. Seven Nation."

"Shit."

"Yeah."

"They're some real nasty individuals."

"Only the worst for my baby sis."

"So, what are you suggesting?"

Ryu drew a deep breath and held it, unsure what to suggest until it was out of her mouth. "We need to find her. I promised Eileen I'd keep her safe."

"Then that's what we do, but how?"

"We find Father RA."

"Who?"

"No idea."

"Should be easy enough to find him then."

"Funny girl."

"I aim to entertain," Indigo said, then fell silent, obviously remembering what they'd just escaped and the reality of the mess they were in sinking in. Ryu could feel her shivering against her side and knew it had nothing to do with the chill night air. Neither girl said anything for a couple of minutes, listening to the sounds of the city down below. There were so many cars on the streets around them it was impossible to tell if the hunters were still down there or if they'd moved on.

"You got your phone?" Ryu asked.

"It's on the nightstand beside your bed. You?"

"Nah. It fell out of my pocket back there. Shattered when it hit the ground."

"Damn."

"No point crying over it. But it means we can't message Talia."

"So we gotta go talk to her."

"You make it all sound so easy."

"Life's only as difficult as you make it, chica."

"Hah! Have you met my sister?"

Ryu knew how the conversation needed to go; *gunmen had just killed Jack and Eileen; come with me if you want to live.* But there was no way she was going to drop that kind of bomb on her foster sister, so she'd need to find some other way to talk sense into her. Which wasn't going to be easy.

"You know where Seven Nation hangs?"

She nodded. "They've got a crib over on the other side of the parkland and corner boys all along that territory."

"So we walk into their patch, say give us our little sis? That's the plan."

"Pretty much."

"Excellent. I love simple plans that are doomed to failure," Indigo grinned, but all Ryu could see in the darkness was Eileen's ghost. She wasn't there. Of course, she wasn't. But that didn't mean she wasn't watching over the girls. "Let's just try and not get shot." The grin, manic as it was in the moonlight, disappeared from her face. "That was a stupid thing to say. Sorry. I —"

"It's all good, Indy, I know you didn't mean anything by it. None of this feels real."

"I'm not gonna argue with that."

"I don't know what I'm supposed to do… I mean… why would anyone want to hurt Jack or Eileen?" But what was going through her mind was how could this happen to her twice?

"No clue. But… you saw them hanging around… this wasn't some random tragedy… it was an execution. So someone wanted them dead."

"Or wanted me dead," Ryu said, following that train of thought to its logical conclusion.

FOUR

With that cheery thought in mind, the girls moved, going from rooftop to rooftop along the street, working towards the park.

It was a straightforward journey during daylight hours, even if it skirted a couple of dangerous neighborhoods, but at night, it was an entirely different proposition. The last thing they needed was to run afoul of the kings of the night, those street boys who absolutely owned the turf, come sundown. So, as much as possible, they stayed out of sight until they couldn't.

It was a vacant parking lot outside a Food 4 Less. Half a dozen cars parked in a ring, all lights on, turning the middle into a stage. Ryu counted twenty-plus bangers sitting on the hoods of the various cars, placing bets as some unfortunate was dragged out of a bare-knuckle fight in the lights against one of their own. It was some kind of justice thing. Money changed hands. The battle was as brutal as it was fast, over in half a dozen punches, and as the unfortunate went down hard. The beatdown didn't stop as he lay on the ground bleeding, with kicks aimed at his head and body with sickening savagery. On top of the hood of a pimped-out ride, a cross-legged figure gave a signal, and the beating stopped.

The bloody unfortunate was dragged away as the onlookers whooped and hollered, and another 'challenger' was carried forward into the ring of light.

Talia leaned up against the side of a Suzuki Samurai. She was smoking a blunt and acting like she was all that, not the jailbait she really was.

"I see her," she told Indigo.

"Hard to miss that little chica," Indigo agreed.

It was true; she was a presence, even as a thirteen-year-old. You couldn't not notice her. She would be a heartbreaker if she lived long enough to grow up. Legs that went on for days developed in ways far beyond her years, with coffee-cream skin and curls.

She looked unhappy seeing her foster sister as Ryu walked towards her.

"What do you want?" Four words, pure venom.

"I don't have the energy to deal with your shit, Tal; I need you to come with me."

"The fuck I will," the other girl spat.

"I'm not asking; I'm telling you; you're coming with me."

"And I'm telling you, I'm not. I'm not a fucking child for you to boss around."

"Then stop acting like one."

"Fuck you."

"They're dead. Jack and Eileen. Two men broke into the house and gunned them down. The last thing Eileen begged me to do was look after you, so get your fucking shit together, we're going." The sheer anger in her tone was all the other girl needed to know she wasn't lying, and the change in her demeanor was immediate and tragic as all the layers of bravado crumbled away, and all that remained was the little girl she really was at heart.

"They're not. They can't be," Talia shook her head. She no longer leaned against the car. She was in arm's reach of Ryu, who stepped forward into her embrace and clung to her for dear life.

"I'm not letting you go," Ryu breathed in her ear as Indigo joined the three-way embrace.

"I don't—why?"

Nothing she said would make sense to her foster sister, so she said nothing.

Instead, she clung on tight.

"As heartwarming as this little family reunion is," the banger on the hood of the Samurai said, "You want to take it elsewhere? I ain't all that interested in your domestic bliss or lack of it, so fuck off out of here before I decide to put the pair of you in the ring and watch you fight."

"Raya, don't be a prick," Talia said, not that he would have been able to understand her for the muffled sobbing and snot bubbles that drowned those five words. "Just gimme a minute to fucking grieve."

"Take as long as you like; just do it somewhere else. All these tears are seriously fucking with the mood. We're trying to have a good time, not get real."

Ryu felt hands on her.

She twisted, trying to shake them off, but the Seven Nation's muscle was stronger than she was, and less than a minute later, all three girls had been dumped back at the edge of the parking lot and told in no uncertain terms to fuck off.

Talia tried to step back onto the blacktop, only to be pushed back, making the message obvious, but she was persistent. The third time of trying, a hand went down to the waistband of a baggy pair of jeans and lifted up the white tee to show the hilt of the gun jammed into it. She got the message.

"You have to ruin everything for me, don't you?" Talia accused her older sister, but as angry as the words were, they weren't aimed at Ryu but rather at the pain she felt inside and couldn't wrap her head around.

Ryu didn't argue with her.

She held her arms wide and said, "I promised Eileen I'd keep you safe. And that's exactly what I'm going to do, even if it kills me."

"Don't even joke about it," Indigo said, shaking her head. "Come on, you two. He's right in one regard; as touching as it is to see you, too, act like sisters, they're looking for us, and we don't want to make it easy for them. We need to get off the street for a while."

"Father RA," Ryu said.

"Who's that when he's at home?"

"No clue. But Eileen trusted him, and that's good enough for me."

"Okay, so we find the good father, who, let's be brutally honest about this, could be anywhere in the world for all we know."

Talia took her phone from her pocket. "Are you always so dramatic?" A few seconds later, she'd Googled the priest's name and found an article about him feeding the homeless in the warehouse district, giving them somewhere to start looking.

The three of them set off across the park, cutting across the pockets of trees. The strip was dying the day kids played frisbee golf until they reached the natural barrier of the lake in the middle, knowing that it would take them hours to get to the warehouse district, even if they ran.

They didn't talk.

There wasn't much to say. It was the three of them against the world.

But then, wasn't it always?

Halfway around the boating lake, Indigo stopped and grabbed Ryu's arm. She pointed. For a moment, Ryu couldn't see what it was her best friend was trying to show her, but as the shadows began to resolve into the shapes of three men, she was left in no doubt.

They'd found them.

Somehow.

Three men came in through the south gate. She couldn't see much in the details but knew from how they moved that they were carrying. They rushed forward with unerring accuracy, straight towards them. It was as if they knew exactly where the girls were.

Exactly.

With pinpoint precision.

GPS.

"They're tracking your phone," Ryu said, realizing that was the only thing they had on them that could betray their position to the hunters. "Dump it."

"Fuck you," Talia said, instinctively. "My entire life's on here."

"I'm serious, Tal, whatever's on it isn't worth getting killed over. Dump it. Please."

"It's not like that shit's not all backed up to the cloud anyway, right?" Indigo said, trying for a conciliatory tone. "It's just a phone. You're not losing anything."

Talia grunted, still unconvinced, but held the phone like she expected it to burn her.

Ryu snatched it from her hand, took three fast strides, and

tossed it overarm, sending hundreds of bucks worth of technology arcing through the night into the lake with a quiet splash as it was sucked under. "I'll buy you a new one," she promised.

"What with? You don't have any money!"

"Come on," Ryu said, dragging them towards the park's north gate.

The girls didn't need to be told twice. They set off after her at a run, knowing that the distance between them and their hunters would close much quicker than they'd like. Their only hope was to disappear into the city's canyons, and it wasn't like they could do the same trick again. It would have been wiser to split up and meet up again closer to the warehouse district, but there was no way Ryu was letting either of the others out of her sight. Too many people she loved had died already. She wasn't losing anymore.

Following the path of least resistance, she raced through the rose beds and the dragging branches of the willow trees, those long leaves and thorns slapping at her face and hands as she pushed through. It saved thirty seconds at the cost of the same amount of scratches, some deep enough to draw blood. She didn't slow down.

Out of the park, she did a double-take, scanning the street for signs of more hunters and, simultaneously, looking for some sort of way out where the others couldn't—or wouldn't think—to follow.

The most obvious choice was the subway, but going down there meant risking getting cornered and, with no way out, ending up dead before they'd finished running. But, if they could make it look like they'd gone down there… with that in mind, Ryu gestured for the others to cross the street and disappear between parked cars and backyards while she tore her top and made sure a piece of the cloth was snagged and easily visible, laying down as best she could a false trail and hoping the hunters would buy it for long enough for them to get out of there.

FIVE

Desperate to blend in despite their hearts pounding, Ryu kept Talia and Indigo close. Every step Ryu took was a calculated risk, her senses sharpened to a razor's edge. She herded Talia and Indigo towards the exit, forging a façade of casual banter that barely masked their collective dread. To run would be to paint targets on their backs—targets that screamed guilt or wrongdoing. Despite the silent scream rising in Ryu's throat, they needed to blend into the backdrop of ordinary life.

They approached a park exit, a potential gateway to their escape, and Ryu's eyes snapped to a city bus groaning toward the nearby stop. Her heart pounded a tribal drumbeat against her ribcage; her adrenaline surged like a roaring tide. If they could board that bus in time, they'd make their getaway before any would-be captors could zero in. But the 'ifs' accumulated, heavy as stones in her stomach. She delved into her jeans' back pocket, her fingers grazing the crumpled ten-dollar bill that signified her only tangible asset. It wouldn't get them far, but far enough to vanish.

The bus was excruciatingly close to the stop now, its mere proximity fraying Ryu's already taut nerves. Time seemed to slow, each tick of the clock a taunting reminder of the gulf between safety and capture. A flash of instinct made Ryu swivel her head; she glimpsed a figure lurking behind them. The air thickened. Was he their pursuer? The gamble was dire, but they had no choice.

"RUN!" Ryu barked, her voice ragged with a desperation she couldn't suppress. She gripped Talia's and Indigo's arms as if she could physically transfer her urgency into them. They accelerated, but not nearly enough. As if triggered by Ryu's internal alarm, the man behind them gave an indecipherable shout, acting as an adrenaline-infused catalyst.

Fueled by sheer panic, they broke into a flat-out sprint, their shoes pounding against the earth like hellhounds were on their heels. Less than a hundred yards to freedom, yet each footfall felt like sprinting through quicksand. A shortcut through tangled bushes and over rusted iron railings flashed across Ryu's mind—quicker but risky, especially with Talia and Indigo. They stayed on the main path, a meager haven in a landscape suddenly turned hostile.

"Don't stop, come on!" Ryu bellowed, unshackling her hold on them to allow for maximum speed.

Just as they neared the exit, a couple strolled into the park, oblivious to the life-and-death drama unfolding around them. Ryu seized this slice of providence, shouting, "Help us! That man is trying to abduct us!"

The woman's face blanched, horror flooding her eyes, while the man pivoted to confront the approaching danger. Ryu didn't linger to see the confrontation; her last glance registered both men squared off in a standoff, buying them precious seconds, maybe minutes.

Their escape path led them to the bus, its engine revving, its wheels already rolling away. Ryu lunged forward, powered by desperation, her muscles taut with effort and strain. The pneumatic doors hissed shut, mocking her with the finality of a sealed tomb. In a move born of utter necessity, she smacked her palm against the glass door. The bus jolted to a halt, and the driver, his face etched in irritation, reluctantly reopened the doors.

"Thank you," Ryu panted, almost stumbling into the vehicle as Talia and Indigo followed. The palpable relief that flooded them was nearly euphoric, an intoxicating contrast to the dread clamped onto them minutes ago.

He was a massive brute of a man with a beard that wouldn't have been out of place in a Peter Jackson movie. He had the barrel chest to match. Ryu began breathlessly recounting their ordeal, but the driver cut her off, jerking his thumb toward the vacant seats while revving the bus into motion. A sudden, urgent thump echoed from the closed doors—another visceral jolt to their nerves.

"That's him!" Ryu yelled, her voice teetering on the brink of hysteria.

"Don't worry, he's not getting on," the driver grumbled, stomping on the accelerator as if he wanted to leave the man far behind. Ryu's eyes stayed glued to the side mirror. The pursuer sprinted alongside the bus, each stride filled with ominous determination, but gradually, he faltered, finally stopping to pull out a cell phone. His eyes remained locked onto the bus until it rounded a corner, disappearing from sight.

Inside the bus, the girls exchanged glances loaded with many unspoken questions and fears. When the next stop buzzed, Ryu felt as though a trap was about to spring; her every nerve screamed with anticipation of some new horror. But when the doors opened, they revealed nothing more threatening than the darkening cityscape.

"How far do you need to go?" the driver hollered back.

"As far away from him as possible, please. You're a lifesaver," Ryu answered, the words tinged with residual fear.

He drove them on, far from the park, before he let them off.

As they alighted, their fare refused, the driver's parting words were a chilling reminder: "Stay safe, look out for each other. The city's full of bad men."

Standing on the curb, Ryu, Talia, and Indigo shook their heads, still riding the adrenaline high of their narrow escape. They were free, for the moment at least, their lives indelibly marked by the harrowing chase and the haunting realization that safety was but an illusion.

SIX

"So where do we go now?" Talia's voice quivered, laced with an unspoken urgency that hung heavy in the air like the scent of ozone before a storm.

Ryu paused, her eyes scanning the labyrinth of streets that sprawled before them. The gloaming sky deepened the hues of graffiti-covered walls and rusty metal, making the warehouse district ahead appear like a landscape from some post-apocalyptic realm. A small semblance of a plan formed in her mind. "We head toward the warehouse district. Fast but discreet. We can't afford to draw attention."

Talia and Indigo stepped beside her, a tinge of excitement lighting their young faces. They whispered and giggled as if this ordeal were just a thrilling detour from the mundanity of life. Ryu clenched her teeth. How she wished she could shake them awake to their peril. But she bit her tongue, preferring their naive optimism over paralyzing fear as long as they kept moving in the right direction.

Every step they took was weighed down by Ryu's hyper-vigilance. She oscillated between scanning their path ahead and glancing behind them at every corner they turned. Though several figures flickered in and out of visibility in the murky distance, the stalker from the park was conspicuously absent. A whispered discussion about hunger and thirst broke out beside her, but Ryu silenced it with a look. Time was an asset they couldn't squander; every stationary second was a step closer to being discovered.

Just as Ryu was enveloped by her thoughts, planning their next move, the jarring sound of her name broke her reverie. Her heart leaped into her throat briefly, and her muscles tightened for flight. But then her eyes landed on a well-known silhouette on a nearby wall: Benny the Hat. The neighborhood's enigmatic wanderer was wearing an absurdly large, beaten sombrero, which he gallantly tipped back, revealing a grin void of several teeth.

"Where're you lot off to? Somewhere exciting?" Benny's eyes twinkled with an inexplicable mischief that seemed strangely ominous in the dimming light.

"We're looking for a guy named Father RA," Indigo blurted, invoking a sharp, admonishing glare from Ryu.

"We have to go," Ryu interrupted, yanking Indigo's arm. "Now." Ryu respected Benny, but even he might unwittingly betray them with loose talk.

Benny chuckled. "Ah, Father RA does serve up a wicked soup; I'll give him that. Maybe I'll see you there." He gave them a wave that was both dismissive and oddly unsettling.

Urgency compelled them forward, their pace quickening until they reached the other side of the road. Ryu felt a shiver crawl up her spine as a black SUV with tinted windows crept by. A grim recognition settled over her. All doubts evaporated when the exact vehicle passed them again a few minutes later. They were being trailed.

"Into that alley. Now!" Ryu commanded, her voice barely above a whisper yet ringing with authority.

No questions were asked. They knew the drill. But as they rushed into the dank, narrow space between old brick buildings, car doors slamming shut reverberated in the tense air, amplifying their heartbeats and the moment's gravity.

They dashed like hunted animals, the waning light casting grotesque shadows on the ground, turning innocuous objects into imagined threats.

No one spoke; there wasn't any need. The atmosphere was thick with a taut, almost palpable fear that rendered words useless. The sound of car doors slamming reverberated through the alleyway like the portentous claps of thunder before a storm. Each echo quickened their heartbeats and magnified the looming dread.

The girls kept running, speeding through the darkened, narrow spaces, their footfalls frantic and discordant, as if their lives were a movie and the pace had suddenly accelerated to double-time. The air was stifling, thick with humidity and reeking of refuse; it clung to their skin as if trying to hold them back. Meanwhile, a dying sun cast cruel, distorted shadows onto the graffiti-marked walls, turning innocent objects—crumpled newspapers, abandoned bottles—into ominous shapes that seemed to lunge at them as they passed.

Just as they burst into an opening that offered the illusion of freedom, they were met with a chain-link fence that loomed like a monstrous spiderweb. Ryu's eyes darted to and fro, finally spotting a bent post. She signaled urgently for the others to follow her, and they scrambled underneath the fence, their movements a bizarre ballet of desperation.

She glanced back; two men were wrenching their bodies through the tangled underbrush, the brambles clinging to them as if even nature was repulsed by their intent. Their eyes glinted malevolently in the fading light and wore expressions of grim determination that turned Ryu's blood to ice.

Legs powered by adrenaline and terror propelled them forward, the three running like a single organism in eerie synchrony. Though they'd put some distance between themselves and their pursuers, Ryu's instincts screamed that this was a temporary reprieve. Each inhalation felt like inhaling shards of glass, but to stop meant something far worse than physical pain.

They were running toward the sound of muffled voices—a potential lifeline. But before they could pinpoint its source, a door beside them was flung open violently, and they were yanked into a new nightmare. The door clanged shut with a finality reverberating through Ryu's core, sealing them into a cavernous, dimly lit space smelling of rotting wood and oxidizing metal.

Inside, the dark was almost tactile—a physical substance that seemed to reach out with clammy fingers, trying to smother them. Towering crates formed a labyrinthine maze of obstacles. Shadows, darker than the surrounding murk, shifted subtly in the corners of her vision. Ryu felt an overwhelming sensation that they were not alone, that they were being watched by unseen eyes from the concealed recesses of the room.

Gasping for air, they stood in a tenuous huddle. Each inhale was a labor, the musty, stagnant air offering little relief. Ryu's eyes, still adjusting, couldn't discern specific shapes in the darkness, but her skin prickled with the terrifying certainty of a lurking presence. It was as though the walls were closing in on them, encircling them in an ever-tightening noose of impending dread.

A chill sank its fangs into the marrow of her bones—a cold,

visceral recognition that surged from her stomach to her skull: they had dodged one predator only to leap willingly into the jaws of another.

In this stifling, pitch-black void, the only sounds were the ragged breaths they drew and the distant, oblivious hum of a city unaware of the high-stakes drama unfolding in its forgotten corners. Ryu's senses were screaming, her internal alarms wailing in a silent cacophony that filled her entire being.

A new level of fear seized her, a bone-chilling realization coursing through her like an electric jolt: they were not merely unsafe but ensnared, caught in a web woven of their own desperate choices. And in that pulse-stopping moment, confronted by darkness so absolute it felt like a physical weight, Ryu understood that they were perhaps further from safety than they had ever been.

Ryu felt the weight of their vulnerability like never before.

SEVEN

"Silence," the man whispered, the word slithering through the air like a snake in the grass. It was a hushed utterance that paradoxically seemed to resonate in every corner of the pitch-black room, echoing off unseen walls and reverberating through the palpable tension. Ryu felt as if the command had snaked into her bones, not compelling her to obey out of fear but because the sheer authority behind the voice seemed irrefutable.

Outside, footsteps pounded like the rhythmic beats of a funeral dirge, growing louder and then softer, closer and farther away. Ryu held her breath as she heard one particular set of footsteps separate from the rest and make its way toward the door. Her heart lodged in her throat as the doorknob rattled, a guttural sound that seemed to groan in the shadowy abyss. The tension in the room stretched taut like a wire before snapping; the footsteps moved on, fading into the distance.

"Stay here," the man's whisper cut through the oppressive darkness again, delicate yet insistent. Though Ryu didn't see him move, she sensed him drift away like a wisp of smoke vanishing into the night. The air shifted slightly, like the rustle of leaves under an invisible wind, betraying his motion. And then, a door creaked open somewhere far across the cavernous space, allowing a sliver of muted light to briefly trespass into their sanctum of darkness. Ryu discerned indistinct voices in that ephemeral moment—shadowy murmurs that evaporated as quickly as they had appeared. When the door creaked shut again, swallowing the light, the room plunged into an even deeper, almost tangible, blackness. Ryu felt the need to speak, to confirm her existence in this shrouded world, but something akin to dread glued her lips shut.

Time dilated, stretching and contracting in that unlit space like a living thing. It could have been mere minutes or an entire hour; the weight of the unknown made each second oscillate unpredictably. Finally, the door burst open again, and this time, a steady stream of light spilled forth, illuminating what was clearly a vast, nearly empty warehouse, its corners filled with the ghostly echoes of its former life.

"You can come out now," the same voice unfurled the words like a carpet leading toward the light. A lifeline.

With tentative steps, Ryu moved toward the illumination, her fingers tightly interlocking with those of the other girls who had shared her ordeal. Her mind flickered to the men who had been chasing them. Were they waiting in ambush just beyond the doorway? Yet, ensconced in this dark citadel, she realized their options were bleak. Hiding was futile; if another chase awaited them, let it come.

"Be ready to run if we have to," she whispered to the others, infusing her grip with a sense of urgency as they moved forward.

As they stepped into the newfound light, it felt like breaking the surface after a prolonged dive into deep, dark waters. They were greeted by the man who had beckoned them to safety. He was a figure of enigmatic allure, dressed in a long, earthy-brown robe that blended seamlessly with his weather-worn skin.

"Welcome," he intoned as if they had crossed an invisible threshold into a domain entirely separate from the world they had known. "I believe you were looking for me?"

"Father RA?" Ryu queried, her voice tinged with disbelief and a touch of awe. "How did you know we were looking for you?"

With a slow, deliberate motion, he turned his head toward a makeshift dining area. Several people were gathered around rudimentary tables fashioned from giant wooden reels that had once held thick cables. Most people were engrossed in their meals, heads bowed in concentration or perhaps gratitude. But one face was turned toward them, wearing a beaming, almost omniscient smile.

It was Benny the Hat.

"But how did he get here in time to let you know?" Ryu pressed, her voice tinged with incredulity.

"He didn't. He arrived while you were in there," RA responded, an inscrutable expression settling on his face like a veil.

"Then why did you help us?"

"Because I abhor the idea of grown men preying on young girls, let that suffice," he declared, his eyes holding a glint of steel that contrasted with his otherwise placid demeanor.

"But what if they'd been the police? What if we were guilty?" Ryu asked, her voice tinged with a new edge of suspicion.

"Then they would have identified themselves, wouldn't they?" RA's voice was soft, but each word was imbued with a gravity that made them seem carved from stone.

Ryu sensed layers of untold stories and secrets wrapped around this enigmatic figure. She wanted to press him for answers, but she felt they had found a guardian in a world that had turned hostile. An instinct deep within her made her trust him, even as another screamed for caution.

"Our friend Benny has vouchsafed you, although he cautioned that your companions require careful watching—especially the youngest one," RA added, a cryptic smile touching his lips as if he were privy to some divine secret.

"She's at a difficult age," Ryu laughed nervously, as though she were the parental figure and her sisters the wayward children. Thalia did not seem amused as RA's laughter joined hers. It was a rich and hearty sound that appeared to originate from some deep, internal well of wisdom and warmth. Abruptly, though, his laughter ceased as if switched off by an unseen hand.

"So, would you care to enlighten me about why you were looking for me? I gather you are in trouble," RA's voice shifted, becoming a near-whisper with urgency.

Without reservation, Ryu unspooled the nightmare she had lived through over the last few hours, murders, wild flight, and all, not omitting a single detail. It was only as she neared the end of her recounting that she realized she hadn't even told her sister Talia everything that had transpired. Until this point, it had been all about survival; conversation seemed an unaffordable luxury. "The last thing Eileen told me was to find you."

"Interesting. And what would you have me do?" RA asked, his eyes intense orbs that seemed to bore into her very soul.

Ryu hesitated, suddenly aware that she hadn't thought beyond the immediate need for sanctuary. "I don't know. Make the world right," she said, knowing he couldn't. "I don't know who else to turn," her voice tinged with a vulnerability she hadn't allowed herself to feel until now.

"You could have gone to the police," RA pointed out.

"And ended up back in the system yet again, split up yet again?" Ryu countered, her voice bitter. "Indigo has family, a real family that loves her, but not me. All I have is Talia. And I promised her, way back, I won't allow us to be separated again. So, when Eileen said find you, that was what I did."

"You're our only hope," Thalia said, quirking a wry grin despite everything.

RA's eyes held Ryu's for an eternity before he finally spoke. "Then you've done the right thing, my child. I can offer you sanctuary, but you'll have to work hard. This won't be a free ride."

Ryu looked at Talia.

She noted the apprehension in her sister's eyes and a begrudging acceptance that they didn't have much choice. "We'll do whatever we can," Ryu stated, making a unilateral decision for the group. Talia exhaled audibly but said nothing. Ryu knew there would be resistance and arguments, but ultimately, Talia would follow her lead.

"When she says we, she's including me in that," Indigo said, "Even if I'm just the sidekick in the sister shoe." There was no bitterness in her words, just a slow climb down from the adrenalin rush and the onset of shock and the slow sinking in that going home could put her own family at risk.

"That is good," RA nodded solemnly. "Because you all have destinies to fulfill. Even sidekicks. We all do."

His words hung in the air, thick with implications and laced with a mystique that perfectly encapsulated the enigmatic realm they had entered. Ryu felt they had crossed a boundary, out of a world defined by the mundane and predictable into one pulsating with hidden currents and untold possibilities. She knew they were far from safe, yet somehow, they were closer to their true selves than ever. It was a disconcerting realization, laden with an immense weight of responsibility and danger. But for the first time in what felt like forever, Ryu also felt a glimmer of hope, fragile yet resilient, like a lone candle flickering defiantly against the encroaching dark.

EIGHT

Ryu couldn't quite decipher what RA meant by "destiny," relegating the notion to New Age philosophizing. But RA was a lighthouse radiating a sense of security in a labyrinthine world of shadows and vagueness. The idea was comforting enough to follow his directives without questioning.

The warehouse where they found themselves was a sanctum teeming with life's forgotten, its sprawling space partitioned by makeshift curtains of tattered fabric and the detritus of an overproducing society. Cast-off wooden crates and pallets, stacked haphazardly, provided the backdrop. The trio served food to an ever-changing tableau of the city's marginalized, passing through the tenuous atmosphere like ethereal figures in an unsung tragedy.

They stirred mammoth vats of soup and distributed clothing scavenged from a motley assortment of boxes marked 'Donations.' Ryu, Talia, and Indigo plunged into this surreal community service, their previously untested muscles protesting under the workload. By dusk, they were drained to a marrow-deep exhaustion they had never known before.

When night shrouded the warehouse in opaque darkness, pierced only by the ethereal glow of a few suspended light bulbs, the girls found their sleeping quarters. It was a makeshift room that felt like an afterthought, partitioned off in a corner of the warehouse. Nestled atop rickety camp beds and bundled under musty blankets, each carrying countless souls' invisible histories, they surrendered to sleep. The room perched on a mezzanine, offering through grimy windows a twilit view of the warehouse's activities below and the sallow, lunar landscape of the city beyond.

For the next couple of days, their activities followed a cyclical rhythm. They swept the warehouse's labyrinthine floors, sorting through bags filled with humanity's discards and chopped vegetables that disappeared into vats of steaming soup. The absence of Benny the Hat, the man with the formerly luminous smile, gnawed at Ryu. His sudden appearance on the third day was both comforting and unsettling. He seemed altered, his smile missing, eyes lacking their previous warmth. A visible tension, like a dark shroud, enshrouded him. When he left as abruptly as he came, the air felt vacuumed of his presence.

"You're just like your father," said a voice awash in cryptic undertones. It seemed to drift toward Ryu like a wandering mist.

Startled, Ryu turned and found an elderly woman swathed in tattered rags, her eyes carrying centuries of unspoken wisdom—or perhaps unspeakable sorrow.

"I said you're just like your father," the woman reiterated, her voice tinged with a strange nostalgia.

"You knew my father?" Ryu inquired, her voice tinged with a mix of awe and skepticism.

"Of course," the old woman whispered, "and the dragon that haunts him haunts you too. I'll be sure to tell him when I see him next."

The world seemed to split open before Ryu could interrogate the baffling mention of a dragon or proclaim her father's death.

Screeching tires shattered the ambient noise as two black cars with tinted windows skidded to an abrupt stop in front of the warehouse, each leaving inky scars on the gray concrete. A third vehicle arrived just a breath later, barricading any chance of exit.

Men spilled out of the cars—ominous silhouettes backlit by the cars' headlights. Ryu's heart sank; she recognized them. They were the ones—the killers of her foster mother, the figures from whom they had fled in terror through a park swathed in moonlight. How could they have possibly traced them here?

Ryu darted into the warehouse, finding Talia and Indigo still engrossed in the mundane tasks of post-lunch cleanup.

"Upstairs. Quickly," Ryu hissed, urgency constricting her voice into a whisper. "And for God's sake, be silent."

Talia yanked her arm free from Ryu's grasp. "What's the deal?" she demanded.

"Not here," Ryu cautioned, her eyes meeting Talia's in a desperate plea. "Upstairs."

They vanished into the upper tiers of their temporary sanctuary, but her thoughts were very much back down below; the enigmatic references to her father, Benny the Hat's mysterious transformation, and now this—how did these fragments fit into the jigsaw puzzle that had become her life? And what did the elderly woman mean by 'the dragon'? Wasn't that heroin? Was she saying her father had been an addict?

They nestled into a dimly lit alcove tucked away in the darkest corner. It was so well concealed it almost had to be deliberate, partitioned from the main space by timeworn draperies that had once been vibrant but were now dulled by years of collecting dust and grime. Cobwebs stretched like ancient lace across the corners where the walls met the ceiling, a testimony to years of neglect.

Old wooden crates stacked haphazardly to one side served as makeshift shelves, holding an array of forgotten artifacts: faded photographs, rusty tools, yellowed books with tattered covers. In this narrow, forgotten chamber, the air felt thick, laden with the scent of mildew, the aging wood, and the haunting whispers of years gone by. Yet, despite the gloom, there was a peculiar sense of sanctity, as if the space itself had been waiting for them—waiting to envelop them in its aged arms and offer a momentary respite from the chaos unfolding below.

And despite everything else, it felt *safe*.

Ryu felt an inexplicable sense of direction, like a compass needle steadying itself. It was as if an unseen, ethereal, yet compelling hand guided her through the maze of uncertainties and perils. Could it be her father's hand, reaching across the veil of existence to lead her through the darkness? Or perhaps some other spectral force entangled in the mysterious threads of her destiny?

Time, that relentless arbiter of all secrets, would tell.

For now, the three girls held their collective breaths and waited.

In the heart of an unsparing night, the air in their makeshift sanctuary was oppressively stagnant, thick with the stench of mildew. Wooden planks on the walls moaned softly as if sighing under the weight of histories they could never divulge.

Outside, the night erupted in a cacophony of unsettling noises—shouts filled with menace, crashes of furniture overturned. Distant, anguished cries wove into the night air like the melody of a cursed lullaby.

Ryu's sense of foreboding reached a fever pitch; escape was an illusion.

All they could cling to was the hope that Master Ra would shield them from whatever darkness loomed beyond that creaking door.

Ryu ordered her companions to stay silent. Their lives depended upon it, even if the chaos outside would likely have drowned out any noise they might make. Better safe than dead.

They barricaded their hiding place as best they could with a rusting metal filing cabinet that groaned under its newfound responsibility. Ryu's thoughts were a whirlpool of fear and calculation. Her eyes darted nervously, landing on the grimy window. Careful to remain hidden, she peered out.

Across the way, homeless men who had been hunkered around makeshift tables were now forcibly grouped in front of a crumbling building. An ominous and bulky newcomer in the streetlamp's glow stood watching them. The hobos weren't the threat; they were victims of the system like the girls. Ryu's gaze shifted.

Five more figures had cornered Master Ra.

The old man was hunched, leaning against his staff as if it were the last loyal friend in a treacherous world.

Her heart ached at the sight.

He couldn't hope to stand against them.

In their few days here, the staff had become an object of fascination for them. RA used it to keep the younger ones in line but occasionally would share an enigmatic story about it as though it was some sacred artifact.

The window was a testament to years of neglect, with cracked glass barely clinging to a dilapidated frame. Still, this disrepair was an unintentional amplifier, funneling the malevolent conversation outside into the room.

"Where are the girls?" One of the sinister voices snapped.

"What girls?" Master Ra feigned ignorance, his voice frayed with fatigue but laced with resilient courage. "There are no girls here."

"Don't bullshit me, old man. We know they're here."

How could they know? Ryu's thoughts raced. A moment of gut-wrenching clarity washed over her, and suddenly, she understood how Benny the Hat had obtained his recent, inexplicable injuries. He had seen them; he had been visited.

Dread swelled within her. They had miscalculated horribly. They were mice in a trap, and the cats were closing in outside. Master Ra stood outnumbered, with only a handful of volunteers whose most lethal weapon was a soup ladle.

Then, the situation shifted irrevocably.

Master Ra, the aging guardian, stood surrounded, armed only with a simple staff. But within him, the ancient fighting style flowed like a river of power. His opponents, brimming with malice, were about to make their move. It was a standoff of epic proportions.

Then, the situation shifted, shattering the fragile balance. The thug who confronted Master Ra reached inside his jacket with a menacing intent. In the blink of an eye, faster than the swiftest of kung fu masters, RA's staff became a blur of motion. It struck with lethal precision, sweeping the man's legs from beneath him before thrusting into his abdomen. The impact sent the assailant crashing to the ground, his world reduced to a head-smashing collision that made onlookers cringe.

Ryu watched in awe and trepidation as her master displayed the artistry of combat. He had incapacitated one adversary, but others reached for their weapons, their intentions dark and unforgiving.

"We need to get down there," Talia's previously hushed voice broke the tension in the room.

"What do you think we're going to do?" Ryu retorted, her eyes still locked on the unfolding chaos below.

"I can fire a gun," Talia announced.

The room seemed frozen as Ryu looked at her younger sister, seeing her in a new light. This revelation unveiled unspoken histories and concealed capabilities. Who was this person her baby sister had become?

Outside, RA warded off the remaining threats, his staff dancing in the air like an extension of his own will. The would-be attackers were disarmed and subdued, their firearms skittering across the concrete. Watching Master Ra fight, Ryu was awash in conflicting emotions—relief, awe, and a new, gnawing worry.

RA's voice echoed from below, ordering people into action while he checked the incapacitated men for remaining weapons.

NINE

The atmosphere was tense as Ryu and her companions descended the creaky wooden stairs. The grimy walls, stained with years of neglect, seemed to close in on them. The air was thick with the acrid smell of damp wood and something metallic—perhaps fear.

At the foot of the stairs, Master Ra had neutralized their hunters. The three burly men faces twisted in frustrated rage, had their wrists bound tightly behind their backs with coarse rope. They looked like predators restrained but far from tamed. Their eyes, cold and remorseless, locked onto the girls as they emerged into the dim light that flickered from an old, buzzing bulb hanging from the ceiling.

"Fuck," snarled the leader, a towering figure with a snake tattoo slithering up his neck. "You can't keep running, girl. We will catch you sooner or later." His voice dripped with a venomous promise, an unsettling reminder of what their hunters were capable of and how far from over it was.

Master Ra, a tall though stooped man whose years had carved lines of wisdom and authority into his dark face, lifted his wooden staff. It was an ancient-looking thing, gnarled and weathered as though it had its own story.

"Not with a broken leg, you won't," RA countered matter-of-factly. His staff was poised menacingly as if he was about to shatter the man's kneecap. The man got the message. He shit up immediately, bravado stifled.

RA then turned to Annie, a formidable woman with a face like weathered leather, her arms sculpted from years of manual labor. "It looks like I will need to go away for a while if we are to ensure the safety of our girls. I trust you can keep our work going here?"

"Of course," Annie responded, gripping a large metal ladle that had proven to be an unexpectedly effective weapon. Her eyes flicked to the restrained men. "What do you want us to do about taking out the trash?"

RA looked back at the thugs. "Don't worry, I'll dispose of them."

Dispose.

Annie looked concerned. "Where will you go?"

"It's better you don't know," RA said, his eyes briefly meeting Ryu's, filled with a mysterious intensity that gave her chills. He pulled out a cell phone hidden within the folds of his flowing, earth-toned robe. He walked away, his voice a low murmur as he talked into the device.

With her blue-streaked hair and nose ring, Indigo turned nervously to Ryu. "Where do you think he's going to take us? Right now, I think we might be better off going to the police?"

Ryu felt her stomach tighten. "You don't have to come with us, Indy, not if you don't want to," she said cautiously, her eyes scanning the warehouse—its dark corners filled with stacks of old furniture and tarps that concealed God's what. "If there's someone you can go to...without putting your folks at risk..."

"I'm staying with you," Indigo declared, her voice shaky but resolute. Ryu felt a complicated blend of relief and dread. She hugged Indigo, closing her eyes tightly as though that would keep the girl safe. When she opened them, RA was striding purposefully toward them, his robe moving like a shadow.

“Get your things together, ladies,” he instructed, his voice tinged with an urgency that sent another chill down Ryu’s spine. “We will leave as soon as I’ve dealt with these cockroaches.”

“What things?” Ryu felt a hollow laugh threaten to escape her. They had the clothes they’d been wearing, dirty and tattered. Beyond that, they had nothing.

Ryu couldn’t shake off the unsettling image of RA facing down armed men with just a piece of wood and a woman wielding a ladle. It was as if he’d unveiled a hidden part of himself, a power she couldn’t comprehend. But the thing that had been most surprising was that the others had stood by, aware of the untapped force that was Master Ra.

She felt a disquieting mix of awe and fear.

And in that moment, facing the three men who would have done her so much harm if they could, she felt a newfound yearning ignite—a desire to be powerful like him, a weapon instead of a victim.

Maybe then she could protect the people she cared about rather than having to run while the ones watching her died trying to keep her safe.

The sight of RA in the full dizzying choreography of the fight had unlocked something within her, an uncomfortable revelation she didn’t yet fully understand, but she would, in time.

Her distant thoughts shattered as RA returned, phone call completed.

“Get ready,” he said. “It’s time to leave.”

Every fiber in her being told her that this departure marked a new chapter even more unpredictable and dangerous than anything they'd faced. Another 'home' is being left behind. She should have been used to it.

And yet, in that grimy, dimly lit warehouse surrounded by souls as fractured as the world they inhabited, Ryu felt an unsettling sense of destiny.

That word again.

RA's favorite.

TEN

The air was palpably tense, almost like an electric charge, as RA secured the three menacing men in the back of the old sedan. Their leader continued to spit threats and curses like hot coals, each expletive punctuated by another precise jab from RA's intricately carved staff. The wooden artifact harmonized with the aged man's movements, adding a disconcerting note to the scene. RA looked at them one last time, his eyes lingering for a moment longer than comfortable, then climbed into the driver's seat. The rusty vehicle grumbled to life, and he drove away, leaving behind a trail of dust and questions.

Her dark eyes clouded with concern and confusion, Indigo glanced at Ryu. "What are we going to do?" she demanded, her voice tinged with an edge of paranoia. "We can't just go with him, can we? I'm so confused, Ryu. I don't know where to turn or what to think… Eileen and Jack… that could have been us… I get the feeling he's going to... take care of them for good, you know?"

Ryu felt a chill crawl up her spine at Indigo's implication, but it wasn't something she hadn't thought a thousand times since her foster parents had been murdered. "If he wanted to kill them, he could've easily done it during the fight," she said cautiously. "I mean, he was armed with nothing but a piece of wood, fighting against men with guns. Yet not one of them fired a single shot." She paused, her eyes narrowing. The atmosphere around them seemed to thicken. "Don't you find that odd? These men killed Jack and Eileen… so why didn't they shoot? Not a single bullet."

The echo of her own words gave Ryu pause. She began to question the enigma that was RA; his presence seemed to keep danger at bay, but it also brought a sea of unresolved issues and mysteries. Was he a guardian angel or a concealed devil? The men had not shot their guns; suddenly, she found herself wondering if they had been afraid to?

Annie, the stout woman with the ladle, was already back to her massive vat of soup as if a violent encounter with armed men was an everyday occurrence. She disregarded the black car parked a few feet away, its presence a looming, silent testament to the drama unfolding. Newcomers milled around the food line, sneaking furtive glances at the ominous vehicle as they waited their turn.

The unsettling old woman who had claimed a mysterious connection to Ryu's father was nowhere to be seen, and for the moment, at least, Ryu was relieved to let that particular puzzle fade into the background for a while longer.

"Come along, girls," Annie barked, snapping Ryu and Indigo out of their anxious musings. "Make yourselves useful while you're still here. Plenty of hungry mouths to feed."

So, for the next twenty minutes, the girls were absorbed in the kindness of the soup kitchen and the manual labor that kept it functioning like a well-oiled machine. They fetched and carried supplies. The physical nature of it served as a temporary balm to their frayed nerves, directing their focus away from everything swirling around them.

However, Talia could only ever be Thalia, which means being vocal in her displeasure.

Her constant complaints punctuated the stagnant air like pinpricks, increasing the tension that had already settled over the group.

"Why does everyone call him 'Master,' anyway? Riddle me that." Talia grumbled, her eyes rolling.

Ryu couldn't answer. She had found it curious when she was first told to find RA and refer to him as 'Master' rather than Father, but since then, she hadn't questioned it. She handed another box to Talia, who snatched it with annoyance.

Relief washed over Ryu when the distinct sound of an engine reached her ears.

A battered brown car, its paint peeling and exposing rusty battle scars, pulled up in front of the warehouse.

RA emerged from the passenger seat, his robes fluttering in the breeze like the wings of some mystic bird.

The driver unfolded himself from the car a moment later—a young black man with a disarming smile that seemed to stretch across his face, illuminating his warm, brown eyes. Yet, something about that smile seemed guarded, as if holding back a thousand secrets.

Talia's face immediately brightened, her earlier complaints forgotten as her eyes locked onto the driver.

Ryu couldn't help but feel a knot tighten in her stomach.

Frying pan, meet Thalia's fire, she thought.

Ryu couldn't shake off the unspoken realization that she had watched RA disarm a gang of armed men with nothing more than a staff and unerring precision. He had received no help except for Annie and her ladle. Why did these men fear to shoot their guns? Was RA some sort of guardian they were wary of, or was there something more—something darker—that she and her friends were yet to discover? Whatever the answers, one thing was clear: they were stepping into a world laden with uncertainties and unspoken threats. A world that could either be their sanctuary or yet another prison.

"Be ready to leave in two minutes," RA said, walking towards them.

ELEVEN

Ryu's fingers nervously clutched the armrest as the car's engine hummed, sending vibrations through the worn-out seats. They had all crammed into the back, her, Talia, and Indigo, their scant belongings stowed haphazardly in the trunk. The tension in the car was palpable. Talia seemed unnaturally engrossed with Marco, the driver's smile contrasting sharply with the situation. His eyes frequently met hers in the rearview mirror, a cryptic expression clouding his youthful face. It was as if he knew secrets the world was yet to reveal to her. Indigo, meanwhile, sat with her arms folded, her gaze fixated on the passing scenery—her eyes, however, seemed to look through it rather than at it. Indigo hadn't said a word since getting into the car. She simply sat there, looking out the window at the world as it went by.

"What did you do with them?" Ryu finally broke the silence, her voice shaky.

"Do with them?" RA parroted from the passenger seat, his eyes meeting hers through the rearview mirror.

"Those men...," she started, hesitating. The atmosphere grew heavier. "Did you kill them?"

A laugh erupted from RA, his deep voice resonating in the small, confined space. Marco's eyes danced with amusement as he looked back at Ryu through the rearview mirror.

"Interesting that your first thought is to judge these old bones as capable of that?" RA mused, swiveling in his seat to face her.

She shrugged, a tingling feeling crawling up her spine. She

didn't know this man, only that he had disarmed those who wanted to harm them with unsettling ease.

"No, dear girl, I left them outside the police station, immobilized in the car," RA explained, his voice dropping. "And ensured that the police were informed as to the kind of people they were, suggesting they might find interrogation useful in their search for an answer to a recent double homicide."

"And who are they?" Ryu asked, feeling as if she was tiptoeing around landmines.

"I do not know, though I am familiar with their type," he said cryptically. "But that need not concern you now. They won't find you where you're going."

"And where is that?" Talia finally tore her eyes away from Marco, her voice tinged with irritation.

RA looked at her solemnly. "You have a choice. But then, you always have. I'm taking you to a place of safety; that is my promise. However, if you prefer, Marco can drop you off, and we can even provide some money for a brief motel stay, and you can fend for yourself. Though I must warn you—I fear you won't see the end of that week, so it isn't much of a choice."

"What do you mean?" Talia probed, but Ryu jabbed an elbow into her side before she could get an answer.

"Ow! What was that for?"

"For asking questions when you should be listening," Ryu hissed.

Talia's eyes widened. "Why would anyone want to kill me?"

"Because they saw you with us," Indigo finally spoke, her voice icy cold. "They want *us* dead because we saw them murder Jack and Eileen, and whether you like it or not, you're up to your eyeliner in this shit now."

RA just observed, saying nothing, his gaze making Ryu feel like an insect under a microscope.

"We're not running from them; we're running *to* somewhere," he eventually broke his silence. "A sanctuary where you can learn skills that will enable you to protect yourselves, to fulfill your destiny."

"You keep mentioning 'destiny,'" Ryu noted, "What does that even mean? I don't mean dictionary definitions; I'm not stupid; I know what the word means, but what does it *mean*?"

RA's eyes narrowed. "You'll learn in due course. For now, let Marco drive. We wouldn't want to distract him and risk crashing this fragile car?"

The words hung in the air like a heavy mist. Ryu glanced at the worn upholstery and the peeling dashboard. The car seemed as fragile as their futures—ready to disintegrate at any moment.

For the next hour, she fixated her gaze out of the window, her mind wandering even as the landscape transformed from urban to rural. They passed through neglected roads that seemed to have never seen the light of development—crooked signposts, dilapidated houses, and vast fields that stretched into eerie forests. The hills in the distance loomed closer each mile, their towering presence captivating and ominous. Occasionally, she caught Marco's eyes in the rearview mirror, their cryptic expression making her increasingly uneasy.

Her eyelids grew heavy, and despite her best attempts, she succumbed to a fitful sleep—plagued by nightmares of relentless running. Jolting awake to the car's rumbling over an uneven terrain, she was disoriented. Gone were the signs of civilization, replaced by untamed wilderness. They were deep into the hills now; the asphalt road had morphed into a crude track overrun by weeds.

Ryu glanced at Marco, whose eyes again met hers in the rearview mirror, and quickly looked away. He knew something—something she didn't. The same went for RA, and it sent chills down her spine. Uncertainty filled the air, suffocating her with the weight of unanswered questions and veiled threats. It was a chilling reminder that, for better or worse, their lives were irrevocably changed, their destinies uncertain and in the hands of strangers. With each turn of the wheels, the sense of unease intensified as if they were spiraling further and further away from the lives they once knew into a labyrinth of unknown dangers and fateful revelations.

And inside, the instinct screamed that same word it always did: *run!*

TWELVE

Ten minutes later, they pulled into an area tucked into the hillside before opening into a sheltered space where a collection of wooden buildings huddled out of sight from the outside world.

"What the fuck is this place?" Talia demanded as the car came to a halt.

Ryu was a breath from rebuking her baby sister for her language but stopped herself. There was no point in pretending they were something they weren't. Thalia had a mouth on her. That was just who she was. RA didn't seem to care, so why should she?

"This will be your new home, for the time being at least," RA replied.

"How long is 'the time being'? This place looks like a dump… shit, it makes the warehouse seem like a palace," Talia said, shaking her head in disgust.

"It is what it is," RA retorted. "And it will take as long as it takes. I will not have your deaths on my conscience. Let that be an end to it. If you choose to stay here, then you will be thankful."

He didn't wait for a response before he opened his door and climbed out, closing the passenger door behind him.

"His bark's worse than his bite," Marco assured the girls as he killed the engine. "Seriously though, you'll be safe here, and right now, I'd say that's worth slumming it a bit."

"Well, no one's going to come looking for us in this shithole," Talia said, eyeing the cluster of huts and half-grinning.

"It's not that bad," Marco assured her.

"I'll take your word for it," she said, giving him a smile intended to make her look more grown-up than she actually was. "And, if you're around, at least there will be one distraction."

"Not for long," Marco laughed. "The Master has other plans for me, it seems."

"That's a shame," Talia's smile faded a moment before she received an elbow in the ribs from Ryu.

Marco stepped out of the car and rested his arms on its roof, the girls quickly following suit. RA had reached the nearest huts and was conversing with a couple of women who kept glancing over his shoulder in the direction of the car.

Ryu could only guess what they must be thinking at the sight of them, but at least they could stop running for a while.

THIRTEEN

RA gestured for the three girls to join him and the women, and Ryu led the way without hesitation. The other girls, a bit more reluctant, followed a pace behind her.

"Girls," RA introduced, "this is Sarah and her daughter Star. They will take care of you and find you more suitable clothes."

Ryu was struck by the age-worn appearance of the two women. Their skin resembled hardened leather, etched with cracks and wrinkles. Had RA not indicated their mother-daughter relationship, she wouldn't have guessed that one was younger than the other. Both wore simple tunics and trousers of an indistinct color that might have once been white. While Star seemed a touch more welcoming than her mother, it was evident that they hadn't been warned of their visitors.

"You are all welcome," Sarah said, although her eyes did not convey the same sentiment. Mya couldn't shake the feeling that they were seen as unwelcome burdens.

Contrastingly, Star smiled warmly. "Master Ra mentioned you haven't eaten since breakfast. Let's see what we can arrange for you."

The thought of food hadn't crossed Ryu's mind, but she realized she was thirsty. She followed Star willingly as they were ushered into one of the huts. Inside, a rudimentary kitchen awaited them. Though spartan, it was adequate—comparable to the facilities at the soup kitchen they had known.

"What is this place?" Ryu inquired as slices of bread were

cut, and a tray with butter, cheese, water, and glasses appeared on the table.

"What has the Master told you?" Sarah replied.

"Only that we'll be safe here," Ryu said.

"That's all you need to know for now," Sarah responded tersely.

"Mother!" Star interjected, "They deserve more than that, surely."

Sarah shot Star a stern glare, but before anything more could be said, the door swung open, and RA entered. "They do deserve more," he agreed as he sat. He filled a glass with water from the jug on the table. Outside, the sound of an engine rumbled to life, and gravel crunched under tires as a car drove away. Mya sensed that Talia would be disappointed to see Marco go, but she also felt it was for the best. Even in a remote place like this, where safety seemed likely, distractions and lapses in vigilance could not be afforded.

"First," RA began, locking eyes with Ryu, "let me ask you a question."

"Sure," she replied.

"Do you know why those people wanted to kill you?"

She didn't think about it, "Because I saw what they did. Because I saw them murder Jack and Eileen. They won't want me around to point the finger at them." Her words were simple and straightforward as if she were discussing someone else's life. But she noticed that he gave the slightest shake of his head.

"Then let me rephrase the question, why do you think they were killed?"

She hadn't really thought about that. Amid panic and the urgent need to escape, the desperate efforts to stay alive and protect the other girls, the 'why' hadn't seemed all that important.

But it did now.

"I don't know," she admitted.

"She died protecting you," he said, pulling all the ambient noise out of the room with the weight of his words.

Talia broke the ensuing silence. "It's true, isn't it? She died to protect you, to save us. That's why they were there. It was never about Jack and Eileen. They came to kill you, Ryu. And she died to save you."

RA nodded. "Your sister is wiser than she looks. You're a very special girl, Ryu. And those people who tried to kill you know that all too well, even if you don't realize it yourself."

"Okay, and this is where you say I have a destiny again, right?"

"It is," he half-smiled. "And who knows, perhaps, as I suspect, you all do. But to fulfill these destinies, you must fight, which means being prepared."

"Prepared? What the fuck do you mean by that?" Talia interjected. "You going to wind us all up like Ronda Rousey and set us off kicking and punching?"

Another half-smile from the old man. "You'll need to control your temper before I let you kick or punch, girl, believe me. That rage in you will get you killed if you can't temper it," he retorted sharply. "And who knows, perhaps you never will, and it will be the death of you. But that will be on you, not on me. I shall try. I shall give you the tools you need. But only you can control your own mind and body." Before she could interrupt, the old man said, "But enough talk for now; I have things to attend to. Do as Sarah and Star tell you, eat, sleep, and your training will begin tomorrow."

Ryu still had so many questions, but she didn't get to ask any of them.

RA left them without another word.

She glanced at Sarah and Star, but neither seemed surprised by his abrupt departure, making her think it was expected. Talia, on the other hand, was visibly irritated. She was still sulking when the sound of approaching footsteps spiked Ryu's adrenaline and flooded her body with a sudden sense of panic.

A moment later, the door swung open, and half a dozen men entered.

FOURTEEN

"Sit yourselves down quickly now," Sarah said, and Ryu instantly felt a sense of ease. These weren't intruders who came to skin her; they were part of RA's family and lived within this isolated settlement. She used the word family in the same way she always did, not in terms of blood but of bond. These were RA's students, each dressed in the identical white tunics and trousers as the two women. Their attire clung to their bodies, revealing muscles toned from labor. Some had tanned, weathered skin, and others bore visible scars—each mark telling its untold story. Their faces were rugged but youthful, showcasing a mix of life experience and untamed spirit. It was as if they had been shaped by the soil they toiled upon.

All men in their late teens or early twenties smiled at the girls as they took their seats. Their hands, roughened from work, fumbled with the modest wooden utensils on the table. Despite their friendly gestures, their eyes showed a discernible shyness, as if sitting down had become a ritual of vulnerability. It was only after Sarah had given a cursory introduction, sweeping her hand to encompass all of them, that they seemed to settle into a more comfortable state.

"These are Master Ra's students," Sarah said, gesturing at the men but forgoing individual introductions. She evidently didn't see the need for particulars. The oldest among them spoke first.

"They call me Raven," he said, his eyes meeting Ryu's momentarily before settling back into his bowl.

“That’s an unusual name,” Talia interjected, Marco now a fading memory.

“It’s the name that Master Ra gave me,” Raven replied, offering a warm but guarded smile to Star as she handed him a bowl of soup.

“Cool,” she said. “Like a street name.”

“Something like that, though we’ve all left the street far behind. We’ve found a place where we belong—found a family,” he added, his eyes taking on a distant, reflective quality. She recognized a kindred spirit in that moment.

“But you’re not going to stay here forever, surely?” Talia questioned, her gaze locked onto Raven’s. A couple of the younger men exchanged glances, their eyes tinged with a knowing amusement. Ryu wondered how often they interacted with outsiders, let alone with girls.

Raven shrugged, the muscles in his shoulders subtly flexing. “Master Ra says there will be work for all of us in time. But for now, we continue to learn and practice.”

“Practice what?” Talia pushed her way into the conversation.

Sarah slammed her ladle onto the table, the sound echoing sharply, making spoons and bowls dance on the surface. “Master Ra will reveal all you need to know in due time. It’s not anyone’s place to second-guess his plans,” she admonished, and that was them told.

Raven bowed his head and focused on his meal.

The other young men followed suit, their faces a mix of respect and restraint.

Ignoring the skeptical faces Talia was making, Ryu finished

her meal, mopping up the last of the broth with a chunk of bread. She felt grateful and didn't want to be a burden, and knew without asking that Indigo would feel the same. Sarah had managed to accommodate them effortlessly despite likely not having planned for three extra guests. She was grateful for the kindness.

"Are there chores we could do?" Ryu asked. Her question was met with a glare from Talia, but both Sarah and Star smiled in response.

"Of course," Sarah said. "There are always chores. As soon as everyone has finished eating, you can wash up. Star will show you where the well is for water, and while it's heating up, you can make up your beds. I believe you will be staying with us for a little while, at least."

They were assigned chore after chore, each task more physically demanding than anything they had been asked to do at the soup kitchen. They continued to work long after the sun had set, and the boys had all retreated to their huts for the night.

Outside, the air was cooling quickly, and the only light came from the moon, the stars, and the dull glow of the lantern inside the kitchen where Sarah and Star sat talking. Master Ra had still not returned, but Ryu took a moment to sit alone with her thoughts. There were plenty of unfamiliar sounds that she tried to identify—the scratching of small creatures, the snuffling of larger ones—but nothing made her feel instinctively on edge. She felt safe there, even though it was all so strange. She wondered if she would ever see any of her old life again or whether she had given it up for good and would never see any of her friends again. But when she thought about it, she knew that her only real friends were already with her.

The door opened, casting a bit more light into the night. Ryu turned to see Star stepping outside to join her.

"How are you doing?" the woman asked. "This must all be so strange to you."

"I'm fine," Ryu said. "Well, as fine as fine can be, all things considered. But I'll just be glad when I get the chance to speak to Master Ra again to try and work out the mess that's in my head. Though, one question, maybe you can tell me why everyone calls him 'Master.' Is it some kind of religious title?"

Star laughed, although Ryu didn't feel she was being mocked. "You'll understand soon enough," she said, dodging the question, just like everyone else seemed to be doing. Realizing her evasion, Star raised a hand to stop Ryu before she could object.

"Let's call it tradition," she said. "There are places like this all over the world where young people are allowed to leave their old lives behind and find a sense of purpose, a direction, a chance for a different life. Most of them are taken off the streets where they would otherwise drift into a life of crime or worse. All these places are led by someone like Master Ra—a school principal, a father figure, and a friend, all rolled into one. I guess calling him 'Master' is a show of respect."

Ryu found herself nodding. It was hard to disagree with something like that. It made a lot of sense. "Does it work? Do these young men taken off the street find something useful to do with their lives?"

Star shrugged. "I can only speak for those who come through

here. Most stay with us for many years before going into the world to find their own path. But it doesn't suit everyone. A few slip back into their old ways; it was ever thus. Yet, Master Ra believes that it will have been worthwhile if he can lift even one person onto a better path."

"And what about you? What brought you here?"

"Ah, now that's a long story, perhaps better saved for another night. It's late, and you've had a long day. I suspect your friends will also do their best to stay awake until you turn in. No one wants to be the first to fall asleep in a new place."

"It's not like I'll shave their eyebrows off if they do," she smiled. "That's more Thalia's style."

In truth, Ryu had no real idea what time it was, but she knew that only the questions swirling in her head were keeping her awake. She did have one answer, though; in Star, she had found someone who would give her straightforward answers when she was ready to ask them.

Questions that could wait until tomorrow.

FIFTEEN

The sound of voices woke Ryu, and for a moment, she had no idea where she was. She lay still, barely breathing, as she cleared the fog of sleep and remembered the events of the last couple of days. Early morning light was creeping in through the thin curtains, revealing the shapes of the other two girls, still sleeping in their beds.

Talia had already been asleep when Ryu made it to her bed, and while she was sure that Indigo was still awake, she hadn't responded when Ryu whispered her name. At some point in the night, Ryu was sure she had heard Indigo sobbing almost silently. The enormity of what had happened over the last couple of days was starting to sink in. Until then, they had been too busy or tired to think about it.

She strained to hear the voices, sure that one belonged to Master Ra, although it was impossible to make out what he was saying or who he was talking to. She hadn't heard a car return, but perhaps that awakened her from deep sleep. She slipped out of bed in the dim light and silently moved to the door, pressing her ear against it. There was no doubt the man's voice belonged to RA, and he was talking to a woman she was sure was Sarah. They were speaking softly, so she had to strain to hear them—until she heard her name mentioned.

"Why don't you come and join us," RA said.

Her heartbeat suddenly sounded loud at the thought of being caught eavesdropping. Thinking, she wondered if she had only imagined hearing him, but she knew she hadn't. She quickly slipped on the white tunic and pants that Star had left on her bed and went out to see what was happening, closing the door softly not to wake the other girls.

Sarah smiled at her as she entered the kitchen, but it was Master Ra who spoke. "It seems we cannot have a conversation without you needing to know what it's about, so you might as well join us." He motioned to the seat next to where he was sitting and waited for her to take her place.

"I suppose you have questions," he said. "Well, this is your chance to ask them."

He waited, unblinking, as she gathered her thoughts. So many questions raced through her mind, all demanding to be asked.

"Why do you think that Eileen told me to come to you? Why did she think you could keep us safe?" She needed to figure out why she asked that question first. The answer already seemed obvious, but there was always the possibility she had misunderstood something or was missing something entirely.

"Because she had been looking after you at my request," he replied.

The revelation hit Ryu with the force of a thunderbolt, each word from Master Ra echoing in her mind, amplifying her confusion and bewilderment. She felt her thoughts scattering in all directions for a split second as though trying to escape the complexity of what she had just heard.

"But..." Ryu began, her voice faltering, unsure how to articulate the swirl of questions bombarding her mind.

Master Ra raised his hand gently and placed it on top of

Ryu's. His hand was weathered and calloused, each line and wrinkle a testament to years of hard work and wisdom. His touch was surprisingly tender against the youthful smoothness of her skin. "She was keeping you safe," he repeated softly, his eyes locking onto hers as if willing her to understand.

"But it cost her her life," Ryu shot back, the urgency in her voice tinged with a bitterness she couldn't conceal. "She risked everything, her very existence, to keep me safe. But why?" and beneath that, a darker question, one that she needed to understand. "Why were those people so desperate to kill me in the first place?"

Master Ra's face darkened for a moment. He looked away, wandering to where Sarah stood, quietly observing their exchange. When he turned his attention back to Ryu, it was as if he had mentally prepared himself to navigate a difficult conversation.

"I am about to use your favorite word again, child, destiny." he studied her face.

"Of course you are," Ryu responded, her tone tinged with curiosity and skepticism. "So, no more riddles; what do you mean by it?"

"There is something profoundly unique about you, my child," he began, carefully choosing his words. "This uniqueness wasn't merely cultivated in your lifetime. It's a legacy handed down from your mother, and she received it from her mother before her."

Ryu shook her head. "I don't possess anything of hers." Ryu was defiant. Bitter. "No heirlooms, no objects of any kind."

RA chuckled softly. "Ah, but you do. You have her eyes, the

shape of her face, the texture of her hair—you are a living, breathing heirloom."

Ryu felt a surge of excitement, a spark of hope that maybe, just maybe, she could find a connection to her past, to her mother, making her more than just a name and a few photos and memories of stories her dad had told her that she couldn't remember correctly anymore. "Did you know her?" she asked, her voice barely above a whisper, as though fearing the answer.

RA's eyes softened, and he nodded. "Yes, I did. Very well. She was an extraordinary woman, filled with the same latent potential you now carry within you. My role, you see, is to help you unlock that potential, to guide you in becoming the best version of yourself."

Ryu frowned, not fully satisfied by the enigmatic answer. "That still doesn't explain why there are people who want to kill me," she said, growing increasingly frustrated.

"But it does," RA insisted. "These people are afraid of what you could become, of the path your destiny will lead you down. They want to snuff out that potential before it even has a chance to manifest."

Ryu shook her head, unconvinced. "If my destiny is so formidable that it scares them, why not just kill you? If you're the one who can unlock whatever this is inside of me, wouldn't killing you solve their problem?"

A knowing smile spread across RA's face. "Ah, what makes you think they haven't tried? Now that we are together, their efforts to find us will intensify. They know it's only a matter of time before you embark on a path that disrupts their schemes."

Ryu noticed the ambient sounds in the background subtly

changing as he spoke. The soft rustle of bedsheets, the muted whisper of bare feet against wooden floors—the others were waking up. RA seemed to sense this as well.

"We must continue this discussion later," he urged. "Your roommates are stirring, and it's best they remain ignorant of these matters for now. Knowledge can be a dangerous thing."

"But you must know that none of this makes sense," Ryu protested, the feeling of being trapped in a labyrinth of enigmas and half-truths overwhelming her. "Not really. Why would the man who murdered my father let me go if he is one of them and knows people want to kill me? Why not finish the job there?"

Master Ra pondered momentarily, his brow furrowing as though sifting through a complex puzzle. "Are you certain he let you go? Could it not be that you merely escaped?"

Ryu shook her head, adamant. "I'm certain. He specifically said that whoever sent him wanted me alive, at least for now, and told me to run. So, who sent him? Why would he say that instead of killing me when I was six and stopping this whole destiny thing?"

RA sighed deeply, his eyes reflecting the weight of unspoken complexities. "Your questions are valid but not easily answered. The fact that someone wants you alive, even temporarily, suggests plans far more sinister than a quick death. I must consider the implications. Thank you for trusting me with what must be a painful memory." He paused, choosing his following words with extreme care. "For now, understand that you are what some call the Radiant Child. While some people wish you harm, it is important to remember that many more would lay down their lives for you."

The Radiant Child? Ryu thought, incredulous. The title sounded absurd, like something from a fantasy novel. Just as she was about to give voice to another torrent of questions, the door creaked open. Bleary-eyed and disoriented, Indigo strode into the room, her eyes struggling to adjust to the morning light.

The interruption served as a natural conclusion to their intense discussion.

Ryu felt relieved and frustrated, knowing that the thread of their conversation would be picked up later. But so many questions still loomed in her mind, more than before they had begun talking, and each one was a piece of an increasingly intricate puzzle that was nowhere near complete.

SIXTEEN

Ryu needed time to think. Part of her was starting to believe that RA was little more than a well-meaning but crazy old man making things up, telling her some fairy tale to try to distract her from all the rest of it, not least the very real fact that Jack and Eileen had been brutally murdered and she'd never stopped running since. But it wasn't working. If anything, she felt more confused and on edge than before. Not that he'd addressed her questions, at least not in any way that made sense.

Her mind kept snagging on that stupid title—the Radiant Child.

Of course, maybe it was just a case of mistaken identity and that she wasn't the girl everyone had been looking for—not RA, nor the killers. That made a lot of sense, even if it made an utter tragedy out of the deaths of her foster parents. But who could she talk to about it? RA only spoke in riddles, and Sarah was tight-lipped. Anything she tried to discuss with Sarah would no doubt get relayed right back to RA. And what then? Would he judge her for going behind his back instead of talking to him?

She was determined to learn more but would have to bide her time.

Sometimes, she'd come to understand that the best thing you could do in the circumstances was nothing. Just listen to what is happening around you. And that was what she intended to do.

Even before breakfast, the chores began.

Ryu had paid little attention to the rudimentary cooking facilities the day before but soon realized that everything was done on a wood-fired range. While the young men collected and cut the wood, which only seemed visible at mealtime, it still needed to be brought inside. The fire had to be lit and fed throughout the day. The stove served as a source of cooking heat and heating water for washing and cleaning, keeping the building warm at night. Ryu wondered if the other buildings had stoves or if their inhabitants had to suffer falling temperatures at night.

Plenty of other chores kept the girls busy, barely allowing them time to relax or dwell on why they were there.

The young men came and went whenever it was time to eat, but they were far more subdued than when Ryu had first met them. The presence of Master Ra had an interesting impact on their demeanor; none of them spoke while they ate. No doubt RA had heard about Thalia's attempts at flirtation, and words had been had. There was no room for distraction in the sanctuary. That much was obvious. Ryu gave her sister a hard elbow in the ribs whenever she tried to start a conversation with any of the boys, making sure she didn't get them in any more grief.

By late afternoon, their chores were complete—or as complete as they could be when they'd have to do them all over again the next day. It was a fair trade-off. Work hard, and stay safe. She couldn't say the other felt the same way—meaning Talia, who had a rebellious streak a mile wide. Ryu knew she would have to watch her while they worked out how long they would hide in the mountains.

Indigo decided she was too exhausted to do anything more than lie on her bed, which struck Thalia as the smartest thing anyone had said in days, so she went to join her. No one objected.

While Ryu would have happily done the same, she knew she needed to build bridges between herself and the rest of the people in the sanctuary with them, especially if she wanted to learn more. And those bridges were built better without her little sister around.

Master Ra and the young men had gone higher into the hills after the midday meal. There had been no sign of them returning until well after Indigo and Thalia had retreated to their room. But then she heard noises coming from outside and hurried to the window, wondering if someone was looking for her.

"Don't panic," Star said. "It's only the others returning."

"How can you be so sure?" Ryu said, pressing closer to the glass but seeing no movement.

"Because the noise comes from higher up the mountain than below us. Besides, anyone making their way up here would almost certainly make at least part of the journey in a vehicle unless it was a solitary pilgrim climbing on foot."

"A pilgrim?"

Star smiled. "Not all young men who come here were rescued from the streets by Master Ra. Some come because they have heard about the place, usually from someone who has been through the program, and decided it might be the right path for them, too."

"Do many just walk up here?" Ryu couldn't help but think of the drive that had brought them up here and how Marco's car had struggled at times. Someone coming up on foot might have found it even harder going.

"Not many," Star agreed, "but I suspect that far more try and give up before getting this far."

"And those that do get here? Do they stay?"

"Of course, they are the most committed. Marco was barely twelve when he made the climb."

Ryu hadn't even considered the possibility that Marco had gone through the same journey as the others under Master Ra's care, yet it made perfect sense. Something about him suggested he had found a purpose in the world and his path.

She was still considering this when RA came inside.

"Ah, Ryu, I'm glad to find you unoccupied here. At least I will not be taking you away from your tasks," he said.

"The girls have all worked very hard, Master," Star said. "The others have taken the opportunity to rest."

RA snorted. Though he said nothing about the other girls' lack of stamina, what he thought of the situation was clear. "Perhaps it is just as well," he said after a moment. "What I have to show you, Ryu, is strictly for your eyes, at least for the moment. You must not reveal it to anyone. Is that understood?"

Ryu nodded. "I understand."

SEVENTEEN

The Beginning - The Forgotten Pharaoh

A madness had overcome the Pharaoh, plunging the country into chaos and threatening to topple the foundations upon which society was built. Though his name was once known and feared throughout Egypt and its neighboring nations, it has now been erased from history. Not just forgotten but actively obliterated; all traces of him have been expunged, monuments destroyed. Fragments of cartouches have been discovered, but even these don't offer his complete name. The only indication that remains in history is a conspicuous gap in the list of pharaohs and the dates of their reigns.

The worship of the Pharaoh was nearly as important as the worship of gods, but this Pharaoh was not content with such homage. He insisted that he was a god, that his power was absolute, and that he could exercise it on a whim. In war or peace, the lives of others were of little consequence to him.

By tradition, the burial complexes for Egypt's rulers were begun almost immediately upon their accession to the throne. Built by artisans and devotees of the ruler, these workers took great pride in their service, secure in the belief that they would be provided for in this life and rewarded in the next. However, those laboring in this particular complex were treated as if they were mere enslaved people, motivated only by fear. Additional labor was supplied by actual slaves—prisoners of war captured during skirmishes with weaker neighboring kingdoms. These unfortunate souls were worked to death, only to be replaced by fresh captives.

It had been long since the Valley of the Kings had served as the final resting place for pharaohs, but he insisted on taking his place there. He demanded a pyramid more enormous than any others, its marble casing to be highly polished to gleam in the sunlight. Yet, even as the pyramid and its adjacent temple complex rose from the ground, the body count also grew. Each day, carts laden with corpses were wheeled away to be discarded in the Nile as offerings to the crocodile god, Sobek. Sometimes, the river would carry a tide of human flotsam to the delta and the great sea.

In different times, a ruler who amassed too much power might be openly or covertly challenged—either by an army leader brandishing a weapon or by a wise man wielding persuasive words. But not in this era. The generals served with unwavering loyalty, witnessing the terrifying consequences that befell those who showed the slightest dissent. They had seen him burst a man's heart with a mere hand squeeze from yards away. They had watched as he turned a man to dust with a wave of his hand. They had noted the sparkle in his eyes when he did so and wanted no part of that evil gaze. No great orator existed who could rally the people against this ruler. Thus, if salvation were to come, it would be through whispered words in private, spoken in secret places, far from prying eyes.

There had to be a way of stopping him and the power he had amassed. It took a little while for a group of men to come together, meeting secretly to discuss what needed to be done and drawing on each other's strengths. Among them were priests, wise men, architects, and magic practitioners, each bringing different skills and representing various possibilities. However, to bring down the

Pharaoh, they needed to find out what granted him his extraordinary power. They needed to speak to Khaphet, the High Priest whom the Pharaoh had appointed as his closest adviser and confidant. Even talking to Khaphet was risky; if he chose to expose them, it would spell the end for all of them and possibly extinguish any hope of stopping the Pharaoh. They could not afford to take any chances.

They sent Horeb to speak with the priest. The old man had been an adviser to the Pharaoh's father and was considered expendable by the son, who had established his court, dismissing all the key figures from the previous regime. Horeb was sure that the priest didn't suspect anything untoward about his visit, yet Khaphet remained tight-lipped when Horeb tried to steer the conversation toward the source of the Pharaoh's power. Khaphet might have accused Horeb of disloyalty, but he merely changed the subject every time the conversation veered in that direction. It wasn't anything the priest said that provided the clue Horeb was searching for; it was a charm carved into Khaphet's door. Horeb recognized the spell because his former Master had requested something similar for his chamber—a protection spell to keep a demon at bay. Why would the High Priest need to take special precautions against a demon? There was only one answer Horeb could think of, and getting Khaphet to confirm it might be too risky. Horeb felt he had learned all he was likely to, but now he needed to share his findings with the others before it was too late—if it wasn't already.

The news surprised the other group members as much as it had surprised Horeb, but none doubted its truth. They were now sure about what needed to be done and hoped they were not too late. The real question was how to do it and whether they could succeed.

Doing nothing was no longer an option, not if they cared about the future of Egypt and its people.

EIGHTEEN

Ryu was startled by the sound of someone knocking at the door, and as if caught doing something she shouldn't, she closed the book.

"Food's ready," Star said softly.

"Coming," Ryu responded. She wondered why Master Ra had been so protective of the book, which could easily be dismissed as nothing more than the ramblings of someone's imagination. And yet, she knew she would have to return and read more. It seemed an entertaining story, but what could it possibly have to do with her? And why was RA so keen for her to read it? She put the book back into the gap in the bookshelf and left the room. Dinner passed in a blur. Ryu ate whatever was in front of her, but she couldn't even recall what she had eaten after the plates were cleared. She helped remove the table and wash up, feeling a little guilty that she hadn't assisted with the meal's preparation. While she was putting away the last of the dishes and wiping down the long table, the other girls joined the men outside, laughing and joking with a lightness Ryu hadn't heard for days. Neither RA nor Sarah had objected to them going out to enjoy the evening air, and they, too, had gone outside, leaving Ryu alone to finish her task. As she was hanging the cloth over the range handle to dry, she heard two voices through the open window, and she was sure they were talking about her again.

She stayed back from the window, not wanting to be seen if either of them glanced inside and caught her eavesdropping. When she heard the word 'father,' she suddenly remembered the eccentric woman at the soup kitchen who had remarked that she looked so much like him. She had almost forgotten about her, but now the memory seemed vivid and important. If Master Ra and Sarah were talking about her, why would they also discuss her father? The woman had spoken as if he were still alive; was that possible? When the door opened, she was about to rush out of the building to ask RA directly, and he entered with Sarah close behind.

"Ryu," he said, "I didn't realize you were still in here. I thought you had finished your work and joined the others."

"Just finished," she replied. "I wanted to ensure that everything had been taken care of."

She saw the look between RA and Sarah and was suddenly certain that they had been talking about her.

"Is my father still alive?" she blurted out before she realized she was going to ask it.

RA paused for a moment before he answered. "Your father?"

"Please tell me the truth. There was a woman... at the warehouse..."

"What woman?" RA asked.

"An old woman... one of the homeless. She said that I look like him."

He smiled wanly at that. "Indeed, you do. A lot. It's no surprise that someone would have noticed the similarity. I saw it right away."

"You knew him then?"

"Of course. I assumed you knew or worked it out when I told you I knew your mother."

Ryu tried to remember if he had mentioned it or not or

whether she had assumed that he hadn't. Still, it came as a surprise.

"How did you know him?"

"For the same reason that our paths have crossed. He needed my help."

"Why would he need your help? Let me guess, you thought he had some kind of destiny, too?" It was a more cynical response than she'd intended, but he didn't rise to the bait.

"That is not a straightforward question to answer."

She remembered something else the old woman had said about a dragon. She tried hard to remember precisely her words, but it involved a dragon. She wanted to ask RA if that meant anything to him, especially if he was talkative, but she felt stupid talking about dragons. As foolish as the old woman had seemed to her.

"How much of the book did you read?" RA asked, pulling Ryu from her thoughts.

"Not much," she admitted. "I found it a little confusing at first, but I remembered a few things we did at school about the Ancient Egyptians. I've just got to the part where an old man discovers that the High Priest had some protective charm carved into his door."

If you read more, things will make more sense.

"But what about my father?"

"It might help you make sense of him, too. Go back into my room and read to the end of that section. When you've finished, we will talk again."

She thought he was playing for time, but she had nothing to lose by reading the rest of the book. It wasn't likely it would take her long, but long enough for the old man to decide what he was prepared to tell her.

He led the way back to his room and lit an oil lamp for her, the smell of it suddenly filling the room. Ryu wondered why they didn't use battery-operated lamps, or better still, have a generator to power the place correctly, but no doubt he had reasons for wanting it exactly as it was.

Earlier, enough daylight was coming through the small window to read by.

"Take your time," he said, taking the book from the bookcase again and setting it down on the table. "I'll be with Sarah in the kitchen when you're ready."

He placed a hand on her shoulder, then patted it—an almost fatherly action.

"Take your time."

NINETEEN

Master Ra led the way outside toward one of the other modest buildings on the hillside. The young men of the compound were busy, carrying lengths of wood that looked freshly cut from trees higher up the slope. A few were breaking them into manageable pieces suitable for the kitchen's wood-burning range. As Ryu passed by, Marco paused his work to smile warmly at her. His transformation was complete, dressed now in the same white attire as the rest. He was no longer an outsider; he belonged here just as much as anyone, if not more so.

"Hurry now, child," RA urged, his voice tinged with purpose. "Time waits for no one." He guided her into the building and along a sparse corridor, finally stopping at a door at the end. The room was simple: a single bed pushed tightly into the corner, a table and chair, a bookcase, and very little else. This unassuming space was, undoubtedly, RA's sanctuary.

"Take a seat," he gestured toward the lone chair at the table before he walked over to the bookcase and selected a particularly worn volume.

"This," he began, tenderly placing the book in front of her, "is the culmination of my life's work. The stories within these pages were penned in tongues as diverse as they are ancient, some translated only recently. This compilation is likely incomplete; tales may have been lost to the ravages of time or may still lie undiscovered in some remote library or museum. Yet, to my knowledge, no other volume like this exists."

He lowered the book reverentially, using both hands as if handling a sacred relic. Ryu felt a certain awe wash over her, a feeling that reminded her of the first time she had seen an old family Bible, its pages yellowed but cherished. Hesitant yet intrigued, she let her fingertips dance lightly over the book's leather binding before summoning the courage to open it. In the ornate handwritten script, read the words on the first page: "The Radiant Child."

"It will take quite some time to absorb all of this," she murmured as she turned the page to find rows of handwritten text, each line a river of thoughts flowing in the eloquent script.

"You don't have to read it all at once," RA said gently. "It's more important that you recognize its existence. This book holds the chronicle of the Radiant Child, a story spanning eons. Due to its singular nature, it must remain in this room. However, you may visit and read whenever your duties and training allow."

"Training?" Ryu interjected, the word pulling her attention away from the enigmatic book.

"You may already be the Radiant Child in essence, but fulfilling your potential—your destiny—requires more than just latent ability."

The word 'destiny' hung between them again, heavy with unspoken possibilities. "But what exactly is this destiny you keep referring to? And why are you so convinced that I am 'the one?'"

"The answers you seek," he paused, locking eyes with her, "are all in here. But you must be willing to search for them."

As he spoke, Ryu realized the depth of his conviction. This was not mere folklore to him. He would not have committed his life to compiling such a vast work if he had any doubt about its truth.

"Maybe I'll read it when I'm less overwhelmed," Ryu finally said, carefully closing the tome.

Master Ra chuckled a warm sound that filled the room. "Given your impending training, relaxation may be a luxury, but I understand."

"Tell me about this training," Ryu urged, keen to unravel more about this supposedly veiled path ahead of her.

"Better if I show you," Master Ra said, his voice tinged with an enigmatic anticipation. "Be ready at sunrise, and you can join the young men."

Ryu felt a twinge of curiosity. She still had no clear idea of the training, but the prospect of glimpsing the lives of the young men in the community held its allure. "I will," she affirmed. Her eyes drifted back to the mysterious book resting on the table, its weighty presence demanding attention. Would delving into its pages cement RA's sanity or reveal an unsettling madness? And what would that mean for her place in this strange, new world?

"And Indigo? My sister?" she asked, her thoughts circling back to her daily life within the community.

"They'll have their duties. Your absence will mean they'll need to work a bit harder," RA responded matter-of-factly.

Ryu knew that would please Thalia no end. But she knew her friend and sister and couldn't imagine either opting for physical exertion over their regular duties. However, engaging with the young men had its attractions—at least for her. She also acknowledged the risk that her absence might breed resentment among the other girls, adding more tension to their already fraught relationships. Yet that was a price she was willing to pay to explore the veiled truths RA seemed eager to share.

"I'll be ready," she reiterated, her gaze settling on the book again. Its leather cover seemed almost to pulse with hidden knowledge as though it were a living entity awaiting her touch.

When she looked up again, she realized that Master Ra had quietly exited the room, leaving her in solitude. She was alone, yet not lonely, for she found herself irresistibly drawn to the book before her. The book's ancient cover featured the symbol of a dragon intricately embossed on aged leather, and its pages held a weathered charm that whispered of centuries gone by. With a sense of respectful curiosity, she opened the cover once more. This time, she hesitated only briefly before turning past the title page. Her eyes danced over the handwritten words, each sentence pulling her deeper into an unfolding narrative that promised to upend all she thought she knew.

TWENTY

The gatherings unfolded like ancient rituals in clandestine corners—timeless and filled with palpable tension. The conspirators sought refuge in dimly lit backrooms of houses that had seen better days, in the sanctum of age-old temples redolent with the scents of incense and devotion, and in the arid embrace of the desert where the constellations themselves seemed to be keeping vigil. Here, in these hidden places, they knew the air grew thick with the gravity of their purpose. To betray the Pharaoh was to court death in its most unforgiving forms, and yet, what they plotted might betray even the gods themselves.

"Does anyone here know how to fight a demon?" One conspirator's voice shattered the silence like a dropped urn, the broken fragments of its question scattering across the room.

Horeb, whose furrowed brow had long been a tapestry of complex thoughts, addressed the room. His words were as calculated as the movements of a seasoned warrior: "It might not be a demon, at least not in the way our ancestors narrated in their tales or the priests depict in their rituals."

He knelt and began to draw on the sand-strewn floor of the chamber, his fingers tracing arcane symbols with the fluidity of a master scribe. The flickering torchlight danced across his face, casting shadows that made his eyes appear like darkened wells. "The charm had something... different about it. Something that does not belong in our known lexicon of spells or curses."

"A flying serpent?" The scribe's voice was tinged with disbelief and something like hope as he leaned closer to the sand drawing. His aged eyes, straining in the wavering torchlight, sought affirmation. "Can this be true?"

"Or a dragon," another conspirator threw in, his voice barely above a whisper, as though the word might betray them. "Though I confess, I have not seen such a symbol inscribed anywhere in decades—perhaps even in a lifetime."

Skepticism rippled through the assembly. "Are you sure, Horeb? Are you certain of what you saw? Could your eyes have betrayed you?"

Shaking his head with quiet but unshakable conviction, Horeb felt anchored by his certainty. This was not a mere lapse in observation; it was an abyss into which he had stared and found staring back at him a truth too unsettling to comprehend. He had also noted the eerie flash of green that flickered in the Pharaoh's eyes when the ruler had unfurled his mystical powers. This was no mere trick of light or shadow.

As the room broke into a babel of hushed speculation and disbelief, Horeb retreated into the labyrinth of his thoughts. A notion—slippery and elusive—fluttered at the edge of his conscious mind, evading capture like a desert mirage.

And then, like a hunter ensnaring elusive prey, his mind gripped the thought firmly. "The High Priest fears a dragon; there's no shadow of doubt about that," he began, pausing for dramatic effect. The atmosphere felt electric, as though the very walls of the chamber were closing in to listen. "Meanwhile, Egypt, and perhaps lands beyond our imagination, live in the chilling shadow of the Pharaoh's might, paralyzed by a terror as old as the sands we stand on."

Another pause. The room, now almost stifling in its anticipation, waited. "The dragon that the High Priest wishes to defend himself against is the Pharaoh. They are not separate—they are the same."

A silence, profound and dense, descended upon the room. It was as if time had stopped to weigh the implications of Horeb's words. Whispers eventually broke the stillness, their low murmurings spreading like fire through dry grass, each man seeking affirmation from his neighbor. Was Horeb's revelation an epiphany or a madman's rambling?

"How does this new understanding serve us?" emerged a voice, carrying a note of vulnerability its owner had perhaps not intended. "Does it guide us toward neutralizing this 'dragon'? Could there be rituals, spells, or anything to expel this entity from the Pharaoh's body and save the bloodline that rules us?"

Faces turned towards Horeb, their eyes like burning coals in the dimness, aflame with a blend of hope, dread, and thirst for knowledge. Horeb met their gaze but found no more wisdom to offer. This enigma was a labyrinth from which not even he could find an exit.

"We must consult someone else," Horeb finally said, his voice low yet resounding, imbued with a gravitas that belied his inner turmoil.

As the words hung in the air, they all sensed the weight of the path ahead—an uncharted course through treacherous waters. They were no longer merely conspirators in a plot against a ruler but seekers on a quest that might take them to the edge of the known world and beyond, into realms unspoken in even the most arcane of their texts. In that hushed room, they understood that their conspiracy had become something else entirely: a pilgrimage into the unfathomable.

"Some else?" came a voice tinged with doubt and apprehension. "Surely the more we bring into this conspiracy, the more likely we will be discovered?"

Murmurs of agreement spread like ripples in a pond, each adding to a growing undercurrent of concern. However, no one seemed eager to challenge Horeb directly. Finally, the Pharaoh's chief architect spoke up. "Who do you think we should turn to that could offer something that one of us could not?"

"The Priestess of Hathor," Horeb declared.

"It will take more than a simple offering to stop this man—or whatever it is that possesses him," someone remarked. "What makes you think that this woman holds the key?"

"Because I have seen her in her devotions," Horeb replied, his voice bearing the weight of conviction. "I've seen her commune with the goddess of many realms. I do not doubt that Hathor will act through her. If the gods have forsaken us, then there is nothing we can do. Nothing any of us can do."

Nods of understanding now passed through the room. These men were among Egypt's most learned, but they knew that without divine favor, they were as powerless as the desert sand.

*

Recruiting the Priestess to their cause proved surprisingly straightforward. She had been aware that the Pharaoh was possessed by something powerful and evil. Initially, he might have controlled it, but now it consumed him from within. She knew, just as the other conspirators did that he had to be stopped. Time was of the essence.

Two weeks. Two weeks to enact a plan that would either liberate Egypt or destroy them all.

The chief architect unfurled detailed papyrus scrolls, showing the excavations around the grand pyramid meant to be the Pharaoh's eternal resting place. Mathematicians calculated points of strategy, while sorcerers discussed the amalgamation of their arcane arts. As for Horeb, he would be part of the ceremonial entourage attending the Pharaoh, a position providing him a vital role in their desperate gamble.

*

On the day of the ceremony, the sun ascended like a golden orb, bestowing its first light upon thousands of faces gathered in anticipation. A raised platform had been constructed to hold the Pharaoh's throne, lifting him above his subjects like a god among mortals. Horeb noticed the Pharaoh had gained a formidable amount of muscle since their last meeting; he exuded raw, intimidating power. For the first time, doubt crept into Horeb's thoughts. Could he, growing older and frailer, stand against this formidable being?

The Priestess of Hathor approached, her eyes locking onto Horeb's, signaling him to prepare.

A low, almost inaudible hum started to resonate in the air, growing steadily in volume. As the Priestess raised her offering bowl, the morning light glinted off its burnished gold. The sound seemed to vibrate in unison with her movements as if connected by some divine thread. A collective breath held the crowd in its grasp—a sensation of both dread and wonder pulsated through the masses like a heartbeat. They sensed the imminence of something grand, something terrifying yet possibly miraculous.

The bowl was raised higher, the humming intensified, and the desert air became charged as if ready to transmit a revelation from the gods.

And then, just as the first sunbeam struck the bowl's rim, reflecting a halo of light around the Priestess, Horeb felt it—a sudden surge of energy coursing through his veins, empowering him with a might he had never known. This was the moment. This was their chance to break the chains that had bound Egypt for too long.

He looked at the Pharaoh, his fellow conspirators, and finally at the Priestess. Their eyes met and shared an unspoken understanding in that brief but eternal moment.

It was time.

Every soul present felt the weight of what was to come—a culmination of fates, a crossroads for an empire, a cosmic struggle about to be unfurled. It was as if the world held its breath, waiting for the scales to tip, for destiny to unveil its mysterious design.

As Horeb took his first step toward the Pharaoh, the bowl's contents shimmered, casting an ethereal light upon the crowd. Was it a reflection of the sun or something more, something divine? Only time would tell, and time, that fickle Master, was running out.

The moment had arrived. The path ahead was fraught with peril but also tinged with hope. Whether their endeavor would save Egypt or plunge it into eternal darkness remained uncertain. Yet, as Horeb moved forward, a newfound resolve fortified his spirit. Whatever the outcome, they would face it as one—mortals and gods, men and women, conspirators and seekers—all bound by the inexplicable tapestry of fate.

And so, in the heart of a land as ancient as time itself, amidst pyramids and priests, gods and mortals, a new chapter in Egypt's endless story was about to be written.

The sound escalated, its vibration seeping through the earth beneath them. Unease infiltrated the crowd, tearing at the fragile tapestry of their collective awe. As a chunk of masonry tumbled from a nearby scaffold, a scream tore through the morning air, igniting a wave of panic that swept across the gathered masses. People trampled over one another in a frantic escape, their fears amplified into a single cacophony of terror.

The Pharaoh glanced around, visibly bewildered. Yet Horeb and the Priestess remained unfazed, rooted in their places like the pillars of a temple.

Shielded by partially constructed buildings and the chaos engulfing the square, the sorcerers commenced their incantations. A sudden flare of lightning shattered the sky, and dark clouds consumed the morning sun. Intermittent flashes illuminated a world spiraling into darkness, exacerbating the collective hysteria.

Another bolt of lightning fractured the earth. Soldiers tried to corral the mob back into place, but the crowd was beyond control. From order to chaos, the tide had turned irrevocably.

Undeterred, the Pharaoh stood from his throne, waving off advisers who urged him to flee. Their words were drowned out by the crackling electricity in the air and the screams below. Horeb edged closer to the ruler, a mixture of fear and resolution tightening around his heart. The end was near; he felt it in his bones.

With another loud crack, lightning cleaved the ground open. The Pharaoh's platform quivered, splintering into fragments as it, too, yielded to the earth's upheaval. For a brief moment, the Pharaoh appeared ready to counter, his inner force gathering to strike. But Horeb wasted no time.

With a burst of energy, he lunged at the Pharaoh, seizing him in a desperate embrace as the platform crumbled away. Below them, the abyss yawned wide, a chasm in the heart of the world with no room for escape.

The Pharaoh's eyes glowed an eerie green, but Horeb's grip held firm. If he were to perish, he would ensure his people's safety. Their bodies tumbled into the void, the only light emanating from the Pharaoh's haunting glow. As they plunged deeper, that luminescent cloud burst from the Pharaoh and ascended towards the sky, leaving the men to their mutual fate.

And then, as quickly as it had started, the storm relented. Light returned, and with one final, earthen groan, the chasm shut itself, erasing any trace of the ordeal.

All that remained was a glowing cloud that hovered momentarily before condensing. It shrank smaller and smaller until it formed a single droplet, which plummeted into the Priestess's offering bowl with a quiet, resonant splash.

Silence fell over the square, a hush of disbelief and awe. People emerged from their hiding places, staring at the space where their ruler and the gaping maw had once been. Nothing remained except the Priestess of Hathor, standing solitary yet unbreakable, holding a bowl that now contained the essence of their fallen Pharaoh.

A new chapter had been written, sealed by the gods, and executed by mortals daring enough to defy fate.

Egypt would move on, its tale forever altered yet endlessly continuing, like the eternal flow of the Nile—forever the same, yet never entirely as it was.

TWENTY ONE

The light had almost disappeared by the time Ryu stopped reading, and her eyes stung from the smoke of the lamp. She couldn't understand why Master Ra had thought it important for her to finish the story, but perhaps he would tell her now that she had.

She replaced the book on the bookcase and turned down the wick on the lamp until the flame went out, plunging the room into near darkness until her eyes adjusted to the moonlight that crept into the room.

She left the room and made her way back out of the building, headed to the kitchen in the main shack. She was surprised to find that neither Talia nor Indigo nor any of the young men sitting outside with them were still there. She wondered just how much time had passed while she had been alone.

RA and Sarah were still in the kitchen and had been waiting expectantly for her. There was an empty mug in front of RA and a coffee pot on the stove.

"Where is everyone?" she asked.

"They're already in bed," Sarah answered. "The girls could barely keep their eyes open, and it was all they could do to keep asking where you were."

"I bet they loved being packed off to bed so early," Ryu said.

RA looked at her. "Early? It is almost midnight."

"Midnight? That's impossible."

"It's true," Sarah said, taking RA's mug from him and setting it beside the sink. "And now it's time for me to go to bed too. Don't let him keep you talking too long; you're supposed to get up early in the morning."

"Don't worry about that," he said. "We can wait a day to start your training."

"No, we can't," Ryu said. "At least, I don't think we can. I'm not sure why you wanted me to read the story, but there has to be a reason for insisting that I read it tonight."

He nodded. "Another day might not make any difference to your training, but it's important that you at least start to understand."

"No, we can't," Ryu said. "At least, I don't think we can. I'm not sure why you wanted me to read the story, but there has to be a reason for insisting that I read it tonight."

He nodded. "Another day might not make any difference to your training, but it's important that you at least start to understand."

"That story. It must be important for you to have wanted me to read it so urgently, but I don't understand why. It's just some fairy tale, even if you've copied it down from somewhere."

"It's far more than a fairy tale," RA said. "It's history. It's real."

"How can you know that?"

"Because I've seen the original papyrus," he said. "I've seen how it was written down at the time, with orders to erase every trace of the Pharaoh, to obliterate his name from any records. But they couldn't wipe it from people's memories. It might not have been written down immediately, but it must have been not long after."

"But someone could have made it up," she said.

"But they didn't. Besides, there's evidence."

"Evidence? What kind of evidence?"

"The essence," RA said. "The Pharaoh's breath that fell into the priestess's offering bowl..."

"What about it? Breath couldn't turn into anything other than a few drops of liquid, that's all."

"It was more than that," RA said. "It turned into a stone, a small green gem, some of the stories say, but it appears in many other stories. It keeps reappearing, but no one realized at first that it was the same thing in each of the tales, even if it's sometimes in a different form."

"That means nothing," she said.

"When you've read the other stories in the book, you won't think that. The breath still exists."

Ryu still needed to find out if she believed him. Something in the story made her think there might have been some truth, but if there were proof, she would have no choice but to believe it. What she was slowly starting to accept, though, was that RA wasn't some madman caught up in flights of fancy; he thought that what he had written in the book was true. They weren't just a collection of myths and legends but a historical record.

"Then where is it now?" she asked.

"That is something I am sure will be revealed to us in due course."

She suspected that was code for him not having any idea, but that didn't make any of it untrue. But there was too much of it to take in when there were more pressing things that she needed answers to.

"And what about my father? Is he still alive?"

"I don't know," RA said matter-of-factly.

"You don't know? That means he might be. There's a chance?"

"There is, but he has been carrying a great burden."

She didn't care about any burden; she only wanted to know whether he might be out there somewhere.

"So he wasn't killed when everyone said he had been? I saw the bullets… I saw it."

"That much is true," he agreed. "But yes, he survived the attack."

"Then where did he go? And why didn't he take us with him?"

"Because you were safer where you were placed."

"Or maybe not," she said. "If we were safe, then other people wouldn't have died."

He didn't argue, and she knew she was right. She was about to ask him more, but he stopped her.

"It's late," he said. "And you are tired."

"I'm not a child to be sent to bed," she said.

He held up a hand to soothe her. "I meant nothing by it. But remember that if you decide that you do want to start your training tomorrow, you'll need to be up and outside at daybreak. We will not wait for you, even if you are only a few minutes late."

That made her all the more determined, but it also meant that she needed to get some sleep if she were to have any chance of joining him in whatever RA had planned. But sleep was a long time coming as she lay thinking about her father and the possibility that he might still be alive out there somewhere. In the morning, she would push RA and ask for help tracking him down. He had to know someone who might know where to start looking.

And when sleep finally came, her father was there, but so were the men who had come to the soup kitchen in their black cars. They were waiting for them somewhere; not all had been taken to the police.

TWENTY TWO

The sun was already making its presence known when Ryu woke. The other girls were still asleep, just as they had been when she had gone to bed the night before. She hurriedly dressed as quietly as she could and left the room. Star was already in the kitchen, starting preparations for breakfast.

"You're too late," Star said. "They've already gone."

"Gone? Gone where?"

"Higher into the hills," she said. "They'll be back in a couple of hours."

"I'll try to catch up with them," Ryu said, tying her worn running shoes.

"You'll never catch them."

"But they can't have been gone long. It's barely light out."

"Sunrise was almost twenty minutes ago, and they're much faster than you. They also know where they're going, and you don't."

Ryu slumped into a chair at the table, prepared to accept defeat.

"You might as well go back to bed," Star suggested.

Ryu shook her head. "Nah, I'm up now and won't get back to sleep. I'll help you do whatever needs doing."

"Thank you," Star said. "That would be very welcome. My mother went to bed late and needs her rest more than I do."

"She was keeping Master Ra company while I was reading his book," Ryu added. "I was reading later than I thought."

"Ah, that explains a great deal."

"Have you read it?"

"The book? No, I haven't. You are very privileged. It's the Master's life's work or at least part of it. Helping get the boys off the streets is at least, if not more, important."

At first, Ryu hadn't even noticed that they had been talking in hushed tones, not wanting to wake Sarah or the other girls. Their rooms were just a matter of feet away and separated only by thin internal walls. There was no different sound except the early morning chatter of birdsong that could be heard through the open window. The peace was interrupted by the sound of a car engine.

Star and Ryu glanced at each other, both aware of the significance. They would have heard if a vehicle had been approaching, but this was the sound of an engine starting up. Who would be using the car at this time of morning?

They both hurried outside to see the car Ryu had arrived in, heading back along the track and down the hillside.

"Must be Marco," Star said. "Perhaps the Master has sent him on an errand unless he had other commitments he needs to attend to. Still, it's odd for him not to say goodbye."

She shrugged and led the way back inside, but Ryu waited and watched the car disappear out of sight, the sound of its engine slowly fading into nothing.

Ryu was disappointed that the young man hadn't put his head inside the kitchen to say goodbye. There was no way he could have known she was awake, of course, but it felt a little off that, given he'd been part of the furniture here for so long, he hadn't at least given Star a heads up. Maybe he was off on some vital errand, time of the essence, and all that? She started to amuse herself by imagining all manner of important—and increasingly unlikely—things he might have been tasked with.

Breakfast preparations were almost complete before Star suggested that Ryu go and wake Talia and Indigo to ensure they were dressed before Master Ra and the students returned. Star hadn't mentioned Marco again when they had been getting things ready, although she had been more than happy to chat about other matters—matters that didn't seem to hold much importance.

The girls complained about being rudely awoken, even though it was later than they had risen the day before, and many of their early morning chores had already been completed for them. When they had roused themselves and dressed, Ryu could hear voices outside. Master Ra and his charges had returned from their early morning activities. It sounded like they had been running, and she was glad she had failed to join them. She'd never been a great runner, though she could hold her own with Talia and Indigo. She knew she would be left behind by the boys or made to feel foolish for holding them up. Still, she felt guilty for not being out of bed and letting Master Ra down, even if he had said she did not need to join them that morning.

"Where's the car?" were Master Ra's first words as he stepped inside before the door closed behind him.

"Marco took it," Star said before Ryu could open her mouth.

"Marco's gone?" Talia said, her voice tinged with disappointment. "He could have taken me with him. I wouldn't mind getting out of here for a while."

Ryu shushed her. There was more going on here than she had assumed.

"I assumed he was running an errand for you," Star said.

"Did he tell you that?"

"He didn't speak at all," Star said, then glanced at Ryu. "We heard a car engine and went outside just as he drove away. We assumed he was on some errand for you."

Master Ra was troubled. "I do not like this. He said he was feeling unwell and still in bed when we left."

"He was gone maybe twenty minutes after you left."

The others filed in behind him, taking their places at the table, intrigued by what wasn't being said as much as by what was, but none daring to speak.

"Does that mean we must walk if we leave here?" Talia asked, breaking the uneasy silence that had settled over the room.

"Come and help me, Talia," Star said before she could annoy Master Ra with more foolish questions.

But Ryu knew that something was wrong.

For whatever reason, Marco had needed to lie about feeling ill and then snuck out with no word as to where he was going or why.

They were free to come and go as they pleased, though, so maybe he just hadn't thought… or had wanted to go down to the Rite-Aid to get some meds to help with whatever was wrong with him?

But then, why lie?

If Master Ra was concerned, then Ryu was, too.

For much of the day, she looked down the hillside for dust trails or other signs of someone driving up toward them, be it Marco's beat-up old car or one of the black SUVs with tinted windows.

TWENTY THREE

Ryu followed him inside, slack-jawed, as he lit one lamp after another to reveal a corridor that led deep into the vastness of the hillside.

"This is why we built the temple here," he said. "Far away from prying eyes."

"But..."

"The caves were already here, though we had to work to make them fit for our use."

Ryu barely heard what he was saying; she was so captivated by the sheer size of the space that had been revealed. One area led to another, effectively creating separate rooms.

"Each of these spaces holds a challenge, a test of mind and body. When you can complete them all, your training will be complete."

"What do I have to do first?" Ryu asked. "All I want to learn is how to fight like you."

"There is no set order. You get to choose which you want to do first."

"Which is the hardest?"

"The hardest? Why do you want to know what the hardest is?"

"Humor me," Ryu said.

"Trying to take shortcuts is not the answer. What might be the hardest for one person need not be the hardest for another."

Ryu shrugged. "Then tell me what you think is the hardest."

He thought momentarily before taking the lit lantern and

leading the way to one of the darkened chambers.

"This test might seem simple," he said, "but it is a test of strength, balance, hearing, and ingenuity."

All the room contained were two upturned buckets standing ten or so feet apart. On the floor beside one of them was a length of thick bamboo with a leather bag fixed to one end.

"Think you could use that thing to knock me off one bucket while you stand on the other?"

"Is that it? Is that the test? The hardest one?"

"It's not as easy as it looks. If I survive for two minutes, you fail. If you fall off your bucket, you fail. If the bag touches the ground, you lose. If you drop the stick, you lose. Understand?"

"Doesn't sound that hard," Ryu said.

"I'll give you three attempts," he said. "If you fail three times, we do it again tomorrow morning with all the boys watching. How does that sound?"

She stared at the length of bamboo and decided that it didn't look too heavy, and it looked long enough to reach someone standing on the other bucket. She felt sure she could do it, and if this was the hardest of the tasks, she had nothing to fear from the others. "Sounds good to me," she said and went to the furthest bucket and picked up one end of the length of bamboo. It was a little heavier and more unwieldy than she had expected, but she stepped onto the bucket once she had hold of it. She glanced across to see that RA was already standing on the other.

"Two minutes is all you have, remember. Whenever you're ready."

She adjusted her stance a little to make herself as stable as possible, then started lifting the pole.

She couldn't lift it. It felt so heavy, and she wondered what he could have in the leather bag. Might it be a lump of iron? Was this just a trick?

"The longer the piece of wood, the heavier it will seem," he said. She didn't know if he was being helpful or just laughing at her expense. But as she thought about it, she knew there was truth in what he was saying.

She pulled the pole toward her, feeding it under her and dragging the bag along the ground until her hands were halfway along the wood.

"Twenty seconds gone," RA said.

She nodded and took a breath, adjusting her grip before she tried to lift the bag off the ground. The pole bowed a little as she lifted it, the bag slowly rising from the ground inch by inch. The bucket shifted beneath her feet, and she fought to retain her balance. That had to be the hard part, she decided. It would get easier from this point; it had to.

She lifted the pole a little more before she started to feed the pole through her hands again. She could not reach the old man, who watched her, his face expressionless.

She was fighting with the pole, the weight growing heavier with every inch she passed back through her hands, but RA was still at least a yard beyond the reach of the end of the pole.

"That's the first minute," RA said. "Another minute to go."

This time, she gritted her teeth, feeling the urge to tell him to keep quiet, but that would only be a waste of breath. Her arms trembled as she tried to keep the weapon, knowing she could not hold onto it much longer. She raised the pole as high as she could and hurried more of the bamboo through her hands. But it was starting to fall, and there was no way she could hold it for more than a few seconds. So she tried to swing it, hoping the bag would reach RA. Any contact would be enough to dislodge him. If he had fallen from the bucket before she dropped the pole, she would still have succeeded.

She yelled as she put the last effort into the move, her footing becoming more precarious, the bucket tottering beneath her feet. She lost her balance, unable to stay on the bucket, but she hurled the pole at Master Ra. Even as she fell, she saw that he leaned to one side, his hands behind his back, and allowed the pole to pass harmlessly past him.

She lay face down momentarily, feeling useless, until RA spoke.

"Get up," he said. "Try again."

She struggled back to her feet, her arms aching in ways they had never done before. Still standing on his bucket, RA held the pole with one hand, offering it to her. She almost took it from him before righting the bucket and climbing on it again. She knew she would never be able to gain her balance enough to step up if she already held the burden.

"Ready?" RA asked when she seemed to have found her balance.

She nodded and accepted the pole when he offered it to her. He allowed her to take a firm hold before releasing his hold. But the moment he did, the weight was too much for her. She strained to hold on but failed. The pain in her arms and wrists proved too much to bear, and the pole clattered to the ground.

"Do you still think that taking on the hardest challenge was a wise thing to do?" RA said. "All it has proved is that you are not ready for this."

Ryu stepped off the bucket and went to pick the bamboo up again, but she knew it was beyond her. "It's impossible," she said.

"Do you believe that? Do you think it would be easier to be the one trying to remain on the bucket while someone tries to hit them?"

"I do," she said. "That bag makes it far too heavy to handle. For anyone to handle."

"Then let's change places," he suggested. "If you think it will be easier that way."

Even as she walked the short distance to the other bucket, she began to doubt what she had said. RA had already picked up the pole and held it out for her, but then he'd had the bag on his end of the pole, a counterbalance. Besides, all she had to do was lean out of the way of the ball and make sure she didn't lose her balance and fall from her position.

"Are you ready?" he asked once she was steady on her bucket. She hadn't even realized that he had picked up the pole, the bag suspended several feet from the floor. She would have been straining at the effort of doing that, but he was acting as if it was no more of a burden than a bag of sugar.

"I'm ready," she said and focused on the bag, waiting for it to rise. It was a moment or two before it began to move, and she couldn't resist glancing at RA's face, expecting signs of effort, but there were none. He was so much stronger than her.

The creak of the bamboo caught her attention, rather than any movement, and almost too late, she saw it coming toward her head. She squatted down a little, allowing it to pass over her head, the rush of air rustling her hair. She was about to say something when it swung back even faster and, this time, caught her on the side of her head. It didn't come hard, but it was enough to disturb her balance, and she slipped from her perch. She had been close, so close, she was sure of that.

"Again," she said, getting back into place and remembering how much harder her second attempt had been. "He must be tiring, too. Ready when you are."

She watched the bag again, this time paying no attention to RA. The bag was the enemy, not the man controlling it. The bag swung towards her head again, but this time, instead of ducking beneath its arc, she leaned back, allowing it to pass only inches from her nose. Still, she did not take her eye off the ball. It started back toward her, this time coming faster, harder, and catching her at the side of the knee. She cried out in pain. The joint bent, and her weight shifted to one side, unable to maintain her balance on one leg. The next blow was enough to take even that from under her, and she found herself sprawling on the floor once more, this time feeling completely humiliated.

RA put the pole down and stepped lightly from his bucket. He leaned down to offer a hand to help her up. Her instinct was to refuse it and get up, but she accepted it. It showed no hard feelings that he hadn't delighted in her pain. It had all been a game, but it had also been an important lesson. She had seen him fight with no more than his staff, but she hadn't realized how strong he was.

"Enough?" he asked.

"I suppose," she said and accepted the hand. He pulled her up with no more effort than he seemed to have expended on controlling the pole and knocking her to the ground. If she could beat him at this game, she would need to be as strong as him, agile as him, and maybe smarter. She certainly wouldn't be able to match him as things were.

"There is a price to pay for failure," RA said.

"A price?"

"A penance, if you like."

She nodded her understanding. "What do I need to do?"

"In the morning, you'll walk to the bottom of the hill, where we turned off the road when you came here. There, you'll find a pile of large stones. Choose one, anyone, and carry it up here."

"Why?"

"Because it will teach you a lesson and maybe more."

TWENTY FOUR

The other girls had demanded to know where she had gone, but she only told them she had been walking up the hillside to see where the boys trained. They had only asked cursory questions and were not particularly interested in hearing her answers. That evening, she was asleep first, her body aching even though she knew she had done little exercise. She dreamed of going through the challenge again, this time with Billy the Hat—the old homeless guy she suspected had given away their location at the soup market—but still, she couldn't knock him off the other bucket. She managed the pole without difficulty, but it wasn't long enough to reach him.

Somehow, she still managed to oversleep. The other girls were already stirring, so she hurried to get dressed and headed into the kitchen, where Sarah was already working hard.

"What can I do to help?" she asked, but Sarah looked at her strangely.

"I thought you had another task to carry out," she said.

Ryu was dumbstruck; she had almost forgotten about the task that Master Ra had set her, and now it looked as if she had been trying to avoid doing it.

"Of course," she said. "I just meant…"

"Best to go and get it over with," Sarah said. "I suspect breakfast will be over by the time you get back, but I'll be sure to save you some."

Somehow, she hadn't expected that she'd be doing this alone.

She was sure there hadn't been any turnings off the road that might cause her to get lost, but she was sure it was quite a distance. But there was no point in complaining or disagreeing, and waiting until Master Ra returned with the boys was only likely to result in public humiliation. It would be better to pay her penance without complaint. And so, she left the kitchen, started walking, and continued walking.

The walk down was pleasant enough. The track was wide, though a little uneven, with grass growing up the center through lack of use. It would not be hard to imagine nature wiping it clean given time. She wasn't sure why the Master had given her this task, mainly since the temple building was already complete.

It took well over half an hour to get to the bottom, even though, at times, the hill gradient forced her to walk faster than comfortable. Her legs were already aching when she reached the bottom, and she paused momentarily to catch her breath. As she rested, she heard the sound of an approaching car on the highway and ducked out of sight behind some ragged-looking bushes that seemed to be barely hanging onto life. The car was black with tinted windows, not unlike the ones that had brought the attackers to the soup kitchen. Her heart was in her mouth, and she held her breath without thinking about it and stayed as still as she could. It drove on without pausing, the driver not even looking in her direction, and she waited for a few minutes in case it came back. Even when she was sure that it wasn't, she kept glancing around to make sure.

She found the mound of rocks without difficulty, a pile of gray stones that had been there for some time. They were of different shapes and sizes, some small enough to carry one-handed without difficulty, but she knew that if she had taken one of those, it would have meant not entering into the spirit of the task. There were larger ones that she would have struggled to lift, let alone carry back up the hillside. She selected one that required two hands and was of a decent size. Any heavier, and she would be struggling long before she completed a fraction of the journey.

It was easy enough at first; the weight was noticeable but not unbearable. However, as the incline increased, it grew more difficult. She struggled when she reached the steepest part, where she almost stumbled. Before long, she was forced to set the stone down to take a break, her arms burning with the effort of carrying it. For the first time, she realized she should have brought a bag of some sort, which made carrying it easier.

The journey took hours, with Ryu stopping and starting with increasing frequency. By the time she reached the main buildings, she had to stop every few yards, yet she still had some distance to travel. She picked up the stone again and walked a little further before being joined by Master Ra.

"You have done well," he said, but Ryu didn't have the breath to reply. Every ounce of energy was needed to keep moving. He didn't speak again; instead, he joined her on her journey, matching her pace and pausing when she paused.

"If you need me to share the burden, you only have to ask," RA said.

She shook her head. She had no intention of giving up now, especially when she was so close. She slipped and fell, dropping the stone when she reached the steep stretch with loose rocks underfoot. It slid down a few feet, but RA did not attempt to stop it. She took a moment to remove bits of gravel from the skin on her hands before retrieving it, half-remembering a myth about a man who kept rolling a stone up a hill. She tried to recall the story while putting one foot in front of the other, gradually getting closer to her destination.

Eventually, even though at times she was barely making four or five steps before having to set the stone down again, she reached the temple.

"Over there," RA said, pointing to a solitary stone to the side of the building. There had been a stone left over when they had built the temple. She laid the stone down, relieved to be free of her burden, and then dropped to her knees. It had taken far more of her than she could have imagined.

TWENTY FIVE

That evening, Ryu returned to the temple with Master Ra. She was surprised he had brought the youngest boys with him this time. Cal was a shy, fifteen or sixteen-year-old, a thin, wiry sort who spoke little but followed instructions without question. Ryu hoped he wasn't being brought along to see her humiliated again.

"I thought it unfair that you should measure yourself against someone who has spent a lifetime preparing for this. Cal is a better match for you to train with until you are ready to complete a challenge," RA explained.

"Who says I'm not ready for another challenge? Perhaps I should try the second most difficult if that was the most difficult?" Ryu retorted.

"I fear that would be a mistake," RA said.

"Perhaps, but surely, it's my mistake to make."

"Very well," he said, telling Cal to return to their hut. "He will not be needed this evening."

The boy did not seem put out, nor was he disappointed. He accepted his instruction without question and did as he was told. Ryu regretted it momentarily, wondering if Master Ra might have been right in bringing the boy along as some sparring partner. But she was sure she was ready to do whatever was required to pass his test and learn to fight.

RA led the way to a different chamber from the one they had used the day before, where several leather bags, similar to the one fixed to the end of the bamboo pole, were suspended from the ceiling on long ropes.

"What do I have to do?" she asked, eager to get on with the challenge.

"It is a simple task," RA said. "All you have to do is get to the far side, pick up one egg from the basket at the far end, and bring it back without breaking it."

"That sounds straightforward enough."

"In one minute," he added.

That still seemed easy enough, which meant there had to be some catch. The light was dim, but she could see well enough to reach the far end and back. Perhaps Master Ra intended to turn out the light at some point.

"Anything else I should know?"

"Only that some challenges are not as easy as they appear, much the same as most things in life. You have three attempts again, and once more, if you fail, there will be a penance to pay."

She wasn't sure "penance" was the right word for it. Price? Penalty? Both seemed more appropriate. But she had no intention of failing. This time, she would succeed, and then he would have to teach her how to fight like he did.

"So, bring one egg from the far end back here."

"That's correct. If you think you are ready, you may begin."

She didn't need any more time to think about it, so she started going through the hanging leather bags, pushing them aside as she went. They were heavy and took some effort, but she made steady progress. When she reached the chamber's far end, it took her a moment to find the eggs, which were nestled in a wicker basket. But when she turned around, she realized all the bags were now swinging, colliding, and bouncing off in different directions. It was impossible to discern any pattern among them. She had the egg in one hand, trying not to hold it too tightly. With her other arm out ahead of her, she lowered her head and tried to push through them. She was struck from every direction—front, back, and either side—each blow made her stumble and fall. She was fighting against the bags and the clock as if they were alive and deliberately trying to stop her.

She was almost through the last of them but felt that time was almost up. It had to be. So, she pushed on, trying to barrel through the last few obstacles, only for one to strike her on the side of the head, swinging too hard. Her free hand went up in instinct, clutching where she had been hit, just as a second one threw her off balance, and she fell to the ground, her knees landing on the hard stone. A gong sounded to confirm that time was up. The egg was still in her hand, unbroken, but then she was struck one last time. It had seemed so simple and straightforward, yet she had failed.

"Again," she said.

"Of course," said Master Ra. "As we've already established, you have three attempts to achieve your objective for this challenge. But you need to understand that you will not have more than one attempt at the final challenge you will have to face."

"I understand," Ryu said, handing him the egg she had collected.

"Then we just have to wait until the ropes stop swinging. That may give you a moment to think about your strategy for your next attempt.

Ryu watched the way the bags still swung, though the force

that one bag was passing on to the next was slowly diminishing. She was the one who had set the first bag swinging without giving it a second thought. She had created the movement by pushing her way through to the other side. She had made her passage back all the harder than it could have been. Next time, she would be more careful; she would slide between the bags as smoothly as possible, doing her best not to disturb them.

It worked, at least in part. By the time she reached the far wall, only a few ropes were swinging, and they were not causing more than a ripple through the forest of hanging leather bags. It had taken a little longer than her first charge through the barrier, but she hoped it would make it faster going back through with the egg in her hand. She was wrong. As she hurried back, conscious of the need to rush, she pushed through, not thinking that the bags would return to hit her. But they did. Somehow, one of them swung back and caught her on the back of her neck, sending her sprawling to the ground and smashing the egg in her hand.

She had failed again despite having taken the time to consider the challenge and try to find a way through it. There had to be a way of completing the challenge, but she was unsure what it might be. Did she need to be faster between the bags? Stronger to push them aside? The gong sounded again, and she realized how close she had been to completing the challenge. For the first time, she was starting to think that she was not equipped to meet the challenges, that it might be necessary to train to be able to complete them rather than just tackling them with barely a glance at what might be required. The challenges required skills she had not yet acquired or more thought. That may be the answer.

Completing these tasks involved more than skill or strength. The solution lay more in solving a problem than crashing through everything.

"Will you train me?" she said.

"As long as you do everything I tell you to, without question," Master Ra said.

"Of course," she said, receiving a raised eyebrow.

"Very well," he said. "We will begin in the morning when you can train with the boys. But at first light, you can collect another rock from the bottom of the hill."

TWENTY SIX

As dawn's first light filtered through the sky, casting a soft pink and purple hue over the world, Ryu set off. The dew-covered grass beneath her feet felt cool, and the air was tinged with the earthy scent of morning. With each step down the hillside, the gravel crunched in a rhythmic pattern, adding to the meditative calm. Today's journey seemed quicker and smoother, almost as if the land was becoming familiar to her. She chose a rock subtly more substantial than yesterday's; its cold, jagged surface bit into her palms as she lifted it. Despite its weight, she had to set it down fewer times than before. When she finally placed it outside the temple, it landed with a satisfying thud beside its predecessor.

The first rays of sunlight touched the carved stone walls of the temple as she heard the distant murmurs and footsteps of Master Ra and his other followers ascending from their huts. She stood up, her back tingling as she stretched, feeling like every muscle fiber was waking up.

Master Ra arrived, his robe flowing gracefully with each step. His eyes, perceptive as ever, fell upon the rocks at her feet. "You have not eaten breakfast," he stated, the words hanging in the crisp morning air.

"I'm fine," Ryu responded, her voice filled with stubbornness and eagerness.

RA shook his head, a gentle but firm disagreement. "Go and get something to eat," he said, his voice dampening her rising objections. She remembered their agreement—she would do as he instructed without question.

His eyes met hers, unwavering, "Join us when you've eaten."

With a quiet rustle of robes, he turned and led the way into the temple, his acolytes following him like leaves carried by a steady stream. The heavy wooden door closed behind them with a resonant thud, leaving her alone. She sighed and headed towards the kitchen.

Inside, the atmosphere was a stark contrast. The room was awash with scents—herbs, spices, and the lingering aroma of cooked food. Girls were busy clearing tables and washing dishes, their movements fluid but cold towards her. Their laughter filled the air but didn't warm it, the social temperature dropping as she entered. It was Star who broke the icy atmosphere, placing a bowl of steaming oatmeal before her. The oats were like tiny islands in a pool of milk, and a comforting aroma rose from the bowl.

"Don't worry about it," Star whispered soothingly. "They're just jealous. They think you're ducking your chores, leaving them with more work."

Ryu looked at Star, whose eyes sparkled as if hiding a secret. Ryu was about to divulge her morning activities but stopped. She sensed Star already knew.

Star's voice lowered, almost whispering, "Don't worry about washing your bowl. Leave it in the sink when you're done and join the others."

After eating, Ryu made her way back to the temple. The imposing door stood closed, appearing even more massive than before. With a hesitating hand, she pushed it open. The creak of the hinges reverberates in the almost sacred silence that fills the room.

Master Ra was there, sitting cross-legged on a woven mat. Sunlight streamed through a nearby window, casting a warm golden pool around him. He looked like a statue, perfectly still, his breath seemingly held in a moment of eternal tranquility.

"Are you refreshed?" he broke the silence, startling her despite its softness.

"Yes, thank you," she replied, her voice steadying, "I'm ready."

"That, of course, is a matter of opinion," he said. Rising to his feet, he unfolded like a blossoming flower, not a single hand touching the ground for support. "This time, we start at the beginning. You must learn to walk before you can run."

He led her to a separate chamber filled with ancient mystique. A bronze bell hung suspended by a thick rope from the ceiling, its surface etched with intricate patterns. On the floor lay a bamboo pole, one end wrapped in a soft leather bag. A chalk circle was drawn nearby.

"Pick up the pole and stand in the circle," RA instructed. "You need to strike the bell fifty times."

The pole felt familiar yet different as she lifted it—its weight balanced, its surface smooth. Before she could swing, RA moved beside her. With deft fingers, he adjusted her grip, aligning the pole so that it rested snugly in her armpit, and ran along the inside of her arm.

"Try to make it an extension of your arm," he said softly, echoing in the chamber, "a part of you rather than just an object you are holding."

She nodded, absorbing his instruction. Her fingers wrapped cautiously around the bamboo pole, its grainy surface feeling like sandpaper against her skin. The pole's weight was substantial but not burdensome; it felt like holding an extension of herself. "How long do I have?" she inquired, her voice tinged with anticipation and dread.

"There is no time limit," Master Ra intoned, his eyes like tranquil pools of wisdom. "This is not a test of speed but of endurance. I will tell you when you have completed the task."

Raising the pole, she aimed. The room seemed to grow quiet as if holding its breath. It took her a couple of attempts to strike the bell, but when she finally did, its peal resonated throughout the room, filling the air like a sudden burst of birdsong—too loud, too piercing. The bell's vibration traveled back down the pole, momentarily causing her hands to quiver. Master Ra, however, remained a statue of stillness and silence.

She had expected him to count aloud each time the bell sounded, but he maintained his calm. Determined, she focused solely on the bronze bell suspended before her. Its smooth, patinated surface seemed to taunt her even as it beckoned. She lost track of the numbers, each strike blending into the next, the lingering echoes disorienting her sense of time and space. Each reverberation felt like a wave, crashing against the walls before retreating into an ocean of silence. Only to be interrupted again by the next tolling sound. Her arms trembled under the strain, muscles screaming in protest, but she clenched her jaw and persevered. She had to reach that mystical number—fifty.

Finally, Master Ra's voice cut through the thickening atmosphere, "You can stop now."

Relieved, she let the pole fall to the ground with a muted

thud, its impact sending a ripple of vibrations through the soles of her feet. Her arm felt like molten lead, nearly paralyzed from the exertion. She sank to her knees on the cool stone floor, each exhaling a tiny cloud of victory and exhaustion, only to hear Master Ra speak once more.

"And now, with the other arm."

TWENTY SEVEN

No matter how much her muscles screamed in protest, and her joints felt like they were grinding on each other for the rest of the day, Ryu was resolute. The other girls would not bear the brunt of her share of the chores. Her hands, gritty from carrying rocks and wooden poles, gripped the broom as she swept the dirt floor of their shared living space. The scent of freshly cut grass from outside mingled with the earthy aroma inside, grounding her despite the pain.

"So, you going to spill the beans? What mysterious rituals are you doing up there at the break of dawn?" Talia asked. Her eyes, the color of fresh blueberries, were narrowed in suspicion. Both girls stood with their arms folded, their postures a synchronized display of impatience.

"I'm not sure you'd believe me if I told you," Ryu responded, her voice tinged with exhaustion. Her eyes met theirs, two pairs of folded arms creating an almost impenetrable wall of skepticism. Ryu felt she owed them an explanation. "This morning, I had to walk back down to the bottom of the hill, pick up a rock, and carry it back up with me."

"Why on Earth would you do that?" Talia blurted out, her voice almost reaching a pitch of incredulity.

"Because Master Ra told me to," Ryu replied, the words coming out more as a surrender than an answer.

Talia and Indigo exchanged confused glances, their eyebrows nearly touching their hairlines. "Plenty of rocks must lie around here without needing to trek all the way down the hill. Why listen to such a bizarre request?"

Ryu sighed, the air leaving her lungs feeling heavier than the rock she had carried. "I'm doing it because I want to learn how to fight like Master Ra. I want to possess the skills he has to keep us safe if those guys come looking for us again." But even as the words left her mouth, Ryu felt their hollowness. The truth was, she yearned not just to defend but to strike back, to take the fight to those who had forced them into this hidden existence.

Indigo, still not satisfied, nudged for more. "That place up the hill, what's inside?"

The shadows in the room seemed to lengthen as Ryu pondered how much to reveal. The flickering candlelight danced on the rough-hewn walls, casting strange patterns that almost looked like ancient runes. "Master Ra never said I should keep it a secret," she finally said, her voice softer, almost whispering. "So, I'll tell you about the caves; the chambers etched into the mountainside like the lairs of mythical creatures, the solemnity, and ancient wisdom they seem to exude." She left out her struggles and failures, not willing to tarnish the imagery with her insecurities.

By the time she finished her narrative, the last of the evening's chores had been completed. Every muscle in her body felt like it had been through a wringer, and her eyelids were heavier than a blacksmith's anvil. The room's single window showed the descending sun casting a warm orange glow over the horizon.

As they exited, Talia and Indigo seemed to mull over her words, their forms silhouetted against the dying light. They joined some of the boys enjoying the evening air, their laughter and chatter drifting in through the open door like fragments of a world Ryu felt increasingly detached from.

When the door creaked open again, Ryu initially thought it was one of them returning. Instead, Master Ra stood there, his silhouette framed by the doorway like a wise elder in a tale of old. She mustered enough energy to stand up.

"Sit," he commanded gently, his voice rich with unspoken meanings. "There's no more training today. You've done well. Tomorrow, we proceed to the next chamber. Rest now. Tomorrow, fetch another rock, but eat before you join us at the temple."

"Another rock?" she asked, her voice tinged with confusion and fatigue. "But why?"

She had hoped that she had carried her last rock up that hill, even though it had been easier this morning than the day before. It had been a punishment for failure, but today, she had succeeded. She had fought through the aches and pains and rung the bell fifty times, supporting the pole with either arm. She had not failed; she had succeeded.

"Remember our agreement," Master Ra said. "You agreed to follow instructions without question. Perhaps we should stop now if you don't feel able to do that."

"No, no, I'm sorry. I didn't mean—"

RA raised his hand to silence her, the simple motion enough to gain her attention and obedience.

"Rest," he said. "Today was the easiest task. Tomorrow will be harder, and the day after that will be harder still. Sooner or later, you might wish that you had not asked to follow this path."

“I won’t give up,” she said.

RA nodded but didn’t say anything more. He got to his feet and left the room, leaving her to her thoughts and utter exhaustion. It wasn’t long before the exhaustion won, and she headed for her bed. She was asleep long before the others took to theirs. She dreamed of carrying rocks up a never-ending hill to the sound of a bell that rang forever.

TWENTY EIGHT

As the sky shifted from dark navy to a lighter shade of dawn, Ryu set off, her footsteps almost soundless on the dew-kissed grass. The morning air was crisp, tinged with the earthy scent of soil and foliage. Her muscles felt like coiled springs, stiff and sore from the previous day's exertions, but her resolve was ironclad. Her goal was clear: fetch the stone and return in time for breakfast before Master Ra led his followers up the steep hill to the temple.

She arrived back at the communal kitchen, breathing harder but invigorated, rock in hand, only to find them still immersed in their morning meal. The aroma of hot oatmeal and freshly baked bread filled the air. The eyes that lifted to meet hers were mainly surprised, yet Master Ra's gaze remained unfathomable as he simply pulled out a chair for her. The wood scraped against the stone floor, a sound that, in another context, might have earned Master Ra's disapproval.

Resisting the temptation to leave the stone just outside the doorway, Ryu knew that would be tantamount to cheating. The stone itself was innocuous enough, slightly larger than the one from the day before, its cold, rugged surface contrasting the kitchen's warmth. Cheating might have saved her a few minutes but could earn her a much longer lesson in integrity.

After the meal, the clatter of dishes and utensils commenced. Ryu offered to stay behind and assist with cleanup, but Sky, her eyes like shards of blue sky, firmly waved her off. To Ryu's relief,

Indigo and Talia neither frowned nor smirked; their faces were impassive as if they had agreed silently to reserve judgment.

For the first time, Ryu stepped into the temple with the others, and it was like entering another world. The air was cooler here, suffused with the mild scent of incense. The walls seemed to breathe age and wisdom. Three rows of disciples kneeled on worn but clean mats, their backs straight as arrows, facing Master Ra. He stood majestically at the front, his robe flowing like water as he knelt and lowered his forehead to the floor in a reverential bow. The others followed, and for a split second, Ryu felt the magnetic pull to join them in this hallowed ritual. But her task was to observe, to absorb, to understand.

When Master Ra rose, the movement was so fluid it was as if he levitated. The disciples reached their feet in perfect silence, a unity that spoke of discipline and deep focus. RA motioned for her to stay behind, along with a boy she thought was named Tom. His features were youthful, but his eyes were hard as flint, not showing any surprise at being singled out.

RA spoke, his voice echoing subtly in the hushed space. "Our young friend will be assisting us today." Leading the way to the adjoining chamber, a sense of anticipation hung in the air, heavier than the scent of incense. Tom offered a respectful bow, and Ryu reciprocated, unsure of the ritual's significance but wanting to maintain the moment.

The chamber they entered was a compact space, its ambiance made more intimate by leather ropes hanging from the ceiling. These were hooked to the limestone walls, worn smooth by time. In the center stood a lone wooden box. Its brown hue seemed darker, more solid than the buckets she had stood on before. It promised a challenge but also a steadfast platform for whatever came next.

"Please," Master Ra gestured, his hand making a subtle arc towards the box as if bestowing it with an unseen power, "take up your position."

She anchored her feet firmly on the rough, wooden surface of the box, feeling its gritty texture under her soles. Ryu looked up, her eyes meeting those of Master Ra, who stood near a pulley system, ropes and balls hanging in calculated positions. His eyes offered no hint of emotion, just the stoic assurance of a teacher.

"Tom and I will release the balls one at a time," Master Ra's voice resonated, filling the chamber with a sense of gravity. "All you have to do is remain standing on this box. You are free to do anything you wish to do. If you fall off, we will reset the balls and go again until you can remain standing until the last balls stop moving. There's no limit to how many times we can reset. We simply stay here until you achieve the goal."

Ryu took a deep, centering breath. She could feel the cool air fill her lungs as the scent of old wood and leather wafted in the room. Her mind flickered to a previous chamber, remembering how she had tried—and failed—to navigate a similar obstacle with brute force. This time, she knew, would be different.

"The balls will be released every ten seconds," Master Ra added, his hands gracefully touching the rope of the first ball.

Ryu glanced around the dimly lit chamber, its walls shadowy but for the flicker of a few oil lamps. She was ensconced in a circle of a dozen hefty, leather-clad balls, each hanging still for the moment. "Understood," she finally said, her voice edged with resolve. "Ready when you are."

Master Ra nodded. The room seemed to tense as he pulled the rope, releasing the first ball. Ryu's eyes followed its pendulous movement, growing larger and faster as it surged toward her. She noted the metal ring halfway up the rope, calculating its effect on the ball's trajectory. Realizing it would lose energy and eventually swing away from her, she leaned out of its path, her muscles tense but prepared.

The air whizzed as the ball passed her, and she turned slightly to assess its return path. At that moment, Tom released the second ball from the opposite side. Ryu quickly shifted her weight and contorted her body, narrowly dodging the second projectile. Just then, the first ball ricocheted off the second, altering its course unpredictably. Before she could recalibrate, it slammed into her shoulder. Ryu wobbled, feeling the box shift minutely under her feet, her body teetering at the edge of imbalance. She fought for control, muscles straining, but was caught off guard by a third ball that slammed into her side. The impact was the tipping point. With a stifled gasp, she toppled off the box.

Without a word, the room sprung into reset mode. Master Ra and Tom deftly returned the balls to their starting points, the ropes swishing softly against the wooden pulleys.

"Take a moment to think about what you're doing," Master Ra advised, his voice tinged with the wisdom of countless lessons. "Consider the physics when we release each rope."

Ryu nodded, her heart pounding in her chest, but her eyes—now more determined than ever—locked onto the next challenge.

Ryu stood in the dimly lit chamber, her gaze flitting over the worn wooden floor and the ropes that dangled from the ceiling, each holding a leather bag at its end. The air was cool and tinged with the scent of aged wood and oiled leather. Her feet felt slightly clammy against the floor, her body tense with anticipation.

"Do all the bags weigh the same?" she inquired, her voice tinged with curiosity. Her eyes met Master Ra's, which sparkled like obsidian chips in the muted light.

"They do," he replied, his voice echoing softly in the chamber. "And all the ropes are of the same length."

The bags swayed gently as if nodding in agreement, casting shifting shadows on the walls, each appearing as an unassuming obstacle.

"And are they always released in the same order?"

RA chuckled a rich sound that danced around the chamber. "You ask a lot of questions," he remarked, his eyes narrowing with a hint of amusement.

Taking a slow, steadying breath, Ryu nodded. "I'm ready."

With a fluid gesture, RA released the first rope. The leather bag attached to it swung forward like a pendulum, gaining speed as it arced through the air. The atmosphere thickened as if holding its breath, waiting for Ryu's response.

Instead of turning to track its motion, Ryu focused on the space around her. The bag whooshed past her, its movement creating a slight breeze that kissed her cheek before dissipating. Her peripheral vision caught the second bag being released, its distinct arc blending into the choreography of swinging obstacles.

By the fourth rope's release, the first bag had reduced to a languid swing, oscillating harmlessly beyond her reach. The initial tension in her muscles relaxed as she decoded the rhythm of the bags' swings, each a note in a silent symphony.

However, she miscalculated once, then twice, and found herself toppling from her perch on the wooden box, the thud of her fall accompanied by the rustle of ropes and the soft thud of leather bags.

RA's voice broke the silence. "Take a moment to think about what you are doing," he advised, his tone as smooth as polished stone. "Consider what is happening when each rope is released."

The ropes were reset, and Ryu mounted her wooden stage once more. Her mind found the rhythm, the hidden cadence that governed the swinging bags. It was akin to a dance, a ballet of anticipation and movement. She began to move in concert with the bags, her body swaying gracefully, dodging the bags as if performing a well-rehearsed routine. The bags swung by, their energy dissipating into soft sighs of leather and rope until, at last, the final bag came to a stop, dangling lifelessly.

RA's eyes met hers, a wordless acknowledgment of her achievement. "You have done well," he declared, his voice tinged with approval. "We will stop now and continue this afternoon. Please help Tom reset the ropes, then return to the kitchen. The others will probably be there already."

A sense of accomplishment washed over Ryu, settling in her chest like a warm ember. She didn't need overt praise; she had met the challenge, and for now, that was reward enough.

In the depths of the night, Ryu found herself restless, consumed by an insatiable desire to improve, to ascend to the pinnacle of her abilities. It all began this night, a burning determination to be the best, a journey that had to remain hidden, a secret path to mastery known only to her.

Under the cover of darkness, she made her way to the training chambers, where the air was thick with the scent of ancient wood and oiled leather. The room was shrouded in obscurity, with only a solitary oil lamp casting dim, flickering light. It was a place of clandestine practice, away from the prying eyes of others.

The wooden floor creaked softly beneath her cautious steps, but Ryu moved with the stealth of a shadow, her heart beating in synchrony with her purpose. The ropes and bags hung from the ceiling, silent witnesses to her clandestine efforts, waiting to be challenged.

Her nightly ritual began, a graceful dance in the obscurity. The bags swayed towards her, their movements a silent challenge that she eagerly accepted. Undeterred, she pushed herself to the limits, achieving feats that defied the boundaries of human capability.

Her fists became thunderous, striking with precision and power that shattered bricks like fragile glass. She moved with the agility of a mythical being, effortlessly leaping over obstacles, her movements a testament to her burgeoning mastery.

In the hushed night hours, Ryu's training continued a secret odyssey toward her quest for greatness. The flickering oil lamp illuminated her path, and her unyielding determination blazed brighter than ever. This was her secret journey, a solitary pilgrimage to become a true master of her craft.

TWENTY NINE

That afternoon, the air was thick with the scent of incense as they returned to the temple. The muffled sound of chanting monks drifted through the walls. Master Ra, wearing his ceremonial robe embroidered with golden thread, led Ryu to another chamber, accompanied by Tom. The young boy's eyes twinkled with a hint of mischievous knowledge as if he were privy to the secrets of this particular room. A constellation of ropes, each tied to an identical leather bag, hung like pendulums from an intricate track system affixed to the high, shadow-draped ceiling. Each rope and bag was fastened individually to the wall, the leather appearing worn and supple, with an earthy aroma that filled the chamber.

"In the center, you see another box," said Master Ra, his voice echoing slightly as he gestured to a wooden platform. It was visibly higher than the previous one, making Ryu's heart race somewhat at the sight. She had to stretch her legs and reach with her arms to ascend, her hands slightly trembling. Once up, she looked down at the cold stone floor, realizing the heightened risk—this time, a fall would have consequences beyond mere embarrassment.

"Much like before, ropes will initially be released one at a time, at ten-second intervals. Tom will wind the handle, gradually increasing the speed. Your objective remains: be the last one standing when the ropes come to rest."

"I understand," Ryu said, swallowing hard. A thin layer of sweat formed on her forehead. Though she heard Master Ra's instructions, a cloud of uncertainty floated in her mind. Would dancing around, like before, be enough? There was only one way to find out.

"I'm ready," she declared, her voice tinged with both resolve and apprehension.

With a nod from Master Ra, the first leather bag was set free. It sliced through the air, its arc widening as it swung menacingly toward Ryu's face. The leathery surface seemed to glint as it caught the ambient light, and Ryu knew she had to act—fast. Her heart pounded like a drum in her chest; she could either sway away, risking a hit from behind or confront it head-on.

Deciding to intercept, she raised her palm to meet the bag, her skin touching the cool, worn leather. The force traveled up her arm, momentarily numbing it. She barely had time to recover or even check the altered trajectory as the next bag launched toward her, aiming for her midsection.

Guiding it to her left with a quick, firm push, Ryu tensed as she awaited the return swing of the first bag. To her surprise, it didn't come back. Her muscles, coiled like springs, relaxed a tad.

The third bag was on its way, and it felt noticeably heavier as it homed in on her midriff. Bracing herself for the impact, she took a last-minute gamble and twisted her body, letting the bag merely graze her side. Just as she thought she'd cleared another hurdle, the next bag lunged, faster and more unforgiving than the last. Ryu felt her feet slip from the wooden platform and plummet off balance.

She landed with a thud, the air forced from her lungs as if squeezed from a balloon. Her back ached, but what hurt more was her bruised ego. For a moment, she lay there, staring at the labyrinth of ropes and tracks on the ceiling, bathed in the soft, golden light filtering into the room. Her eyes narrowed at the detail: two ropes switched tracks. The complex system made sense convolutedly; it kept the ropes from simply retracing their paths, complicating the task. It also explained why Tom was there, winding that handle.

As if responding to her silent musings, Tom pulled a lever. The two separated ropes rejoined the main track, resetting the labyrinth above for another go. With a deep breath, Ryu readied herself for the next round.

She climbed back onto the box, ready to try again but still feeling the effects of the fall. Seconds later, the first bag swung towards her again, and she pushed it aside, making sure she gave it enough force to shift it to the other track, readying herself for the second. When the third bag hurtled towards her, she raised one leg and pushed it aside with the outside of her thigh, pivoting on her other foot. The temptation to glance up to ensure she succeeded was almost too great; she couldn't afford to take her concentration off the next rope for even a second.

The next rope came faster, and unlike the others, it had two bags tied to it at different heights. She tried to push both at once but failed miserably. It barely shifted from its path and left her unprepared for the next bag, which struck her on the hip. She tried to steady herself, but the following bag caught her square in the chest, and she gave up the fight to stay in the box.

Again and again, she tried, but each time, she failed to deal with the rope with two bags attached. Each attempt took too long, leaving her with insufficient time to deal with the next. She needed more time but could hardly ask Master Ra to give it to her. There had to be a way.

She picked herself up off the ground, a little wearier than before, her left arm sore from landing on the hard stone floor, but she couldn't admit defeat. She had to keep going until she could complete the task.

"Do you need to rest?" Master Ra asked.

Ryu shook her head. Saying she needed a rest would almost be a sign of defeat. She would try again. She climbed back onto the box, pausing when resting on one foot and a knee. With a hand resting on the box, she had found a sturdier base than standing on two feet. It could help deal with the time she needed to manage the rope with two bags, but it could be the start of an idea.

She realized what she had to do when the rope with the two bags appeared next in the queue. As the rope swung towards her, she swayed out of the way to allow it to pass, then prepared herself for the next. One after another, she pushed the other ropes out of the way with one part of her body or another.

The rope causing her so much difficulty still came around too quickly, rejoining the back of the line. She allowed it to pass her a second time, then dropped into a crouch that she thought would give her more stability. When the rope completed its circuit, she was ready for it.

She doubted she had enough strength to push it off its path to join the others, so instead of pushing it, she grabbed the lower bag and pulled it towards her before pushing it away, desperately trying to maintain her balance. The moment she released it, she allowed herself the time to look up and see it slip across to join the other stationary ropes.

She had done it.

She was rewarded with another nod from Master Ra, a subtle but poignant gesture that seemed to emanate wisdom from beneath his bushy gray eyebrows. Ryu knew this fleeting acknowledgment was the only overt sign of approval she would receive.

"Your challenge has been completed," he said, his voice echoing slightly in the stone-walled chamber. "You have the rest of the day to do as you choose. In the morning, you will collect another stone before you face your next chamber.

Another stone. The words seemed to hover in the air for a moment. Somehow, the notion of another stone didn't perturb her as much as it once would have. Yet, she couldn't shake the feeling of a vague injustice; why should she incur another penalty when she had surmounted two challenges in one day? The question hung over her like a low cloud, mysterious and unanswered.

"Can I help at all?" she asked Tom as the young apprentice engaged a series of ancient, rusty levers and turned a large wooden wheel to reset the challenge. The wheel creaked in protest, readying the ropes and leather bags for whoever would need to face this intricate maze next.

"It's okay, thanks," he said, his eyes focused on the mechanical dance of ropes and pulleys. "This was built to be operated by a single person."

"Any idea what comes next?" Ryu's voice was piqued with curiosity.

"Next?" Tom echoed, his hand pausing over the wheel.

"The next challenge?" Ryu pressed, her eyes searching his for a hint of revelation.

"I'm afraid I'm sworn to secrecy, just as those before me were. It would be unfair to have advance warning of anything you will come up against."

"But I already know about two of the challenges that will come at the end."

"No. You've already tried and failed those two challenges," Tom replied, his voice steady as if reciting a well-rehearsed rule. "That isn't the same. No one helped you or forewarned you about what was to come. It wouldn't be fair on everyone else who has been through this."

Ryu sensed the weight of tradition in his words and decided not to challenge it further. "Sorry," she said, her voice softening. "I didn't mean…"

"It doesn't matter," he said, pulling the last lever into place with a resonant clank. "You did well today, but you'll need to dig even deeper for what lies ahead. Some of us gather here after our evening meal; you can join us if you wish."

"Thank you," Ryu replied, her eyes catching a glint of the setting sun as it filtered through a narrow window, casting an amber glow on the stone floor. She felt humbled and intrigued, not knowing what she was letting herself in for. "I would like that."

THIRTY

Ryu wasn't sure what to anticipate as she stepped back into the dimly lit temple, the aroma of incense and aged wood filling her nostrils. The younger boys, their eyes earnest and keen, and Tariq, an older student with a commanding presence, led the way. The flickering lamps cast intricate shadows on the worn wooden floor and ancient tapestries. She wondered if Tom had prepped them about her presence; their faces remained unreadable.

The dying sun outside necessitated the lighting of oil lamps, their flickering flames casting a mystical glow over the chamber. A heavy door to the inner chambers stayed stubbornly closed, its secrets veiled for another time.

"Why don't you watch first?" Tom's voice broke the silence, each word tinged with a cryptic resonance. "Then you can have a try."

She nodded, feeling the weight of the room's ancient wisdom envelop her like a dense fog. Her eyes fixed on Tariq, who stood with a regal dignity at the front of the room. The elegant and fluid movements he began to execute stirred her memory of Tai Chi sessions she'd seen in the park—elderly people moving slowly, meditatively. But this was different; it was like watching the water flow over stones, graceful yet forceful.

Tariq's actions seemed to be encoded into the muscle memory of the other boys; they mirrored him in near-perfect synchronization. The room transformed into a dance of swaying bodies, like leaves, in a unified breeze. They repeated the sequence at a slightly faster tempo, their movements weaving a tapestry of focused energy in the air. Ryu felt magnetically pulled into their rhythm. Hesitantly, she began to emulate their movements, her muscles tensing and relaxing in a hesitant mimicry of their flow.

This kinetic ballet reminded her of a dance, each move a word in a silent language, each sequence a sentence. By the third repetition, her body had internalized the rhythm, the pattern. Tariq beckoned her forward, his eyes locking onto hers for a fleeting moment, and the boys seamlessly parted to give her a spot at the forefront.

"Let's go again," Tariq intoned, his voice capturing the room's attention like a drumbeat, and they immersed themselves into the rhythm once more.

Unbeknownst to her, Master Ra had entered, a nearly ethereal figure in the lamp's glow. He moved beside her, his touch gentle yet firm as he corrected her stance—a lifted elbow here, a slight head tilt there.

They began another sequence. "Close your eyes on the first move," RA's whisper ghosted.

A shiver of apprehension coursed through her. She worried this might be some form of mockery. However, with a deep breath, she trusted and closed her eyes. Her senses heightened; she felt each shift and turn, each flex and release, more intimately than before.

"Now imagine an assailant approaching," RA guided, his words a quiet breeze through her heightened awareness.

In her mind's eye, a menacing figure materialized—the

haunting visage of Eileen and Jack's killer. She had never seen him, but she knew this was the gunman. His fist swung at her; her left hand deflected it, the motion as natural as exhaling. Her right hand, now a taut weapon, lunged into his stomach with a force that seemed to steal his breath. Pivoting, she felt her leg extend like a whip, touching his knees. A muffled scream escaped his lips. In one fluid motion, the heel of her hand met his face. A sense of invigorating triumph surged through her, pulling a satisfied smile onto her lips.

"You can open your eyes now," the timbre of Master Ra's voice brought her back into the room, back into her own body, but forever changed.

It took a conscious effort for Ryu to halt the kinetic energy flowing through her limbs. Even in her ephemeral moments in the temple, the choreographed movements seemed to awaken slumbering muscle memories deep within her. Her gaze swept across the room, meeting no one's eyes. The boys were entranced in their own fluid motions, their focus laser-sharp, as if the rest of the world had blurred away. The air was thick with the scent of perspiration and aged wood from the temple's ancient pillars. Ryu wondered if their minds were also filled with phantom adversaries.

With an authoritative clap that resonated like a gong, Master Ra signaled the end of the cycle. The echo of his clap hung in the air as all the students instantly froze their movements and aligned their bodies in an erect stance. The room grew quiet, punctuated only by the unified sounds of inhaling and exhaling. Ryu mimicked their posture, her mind abuzz with electric possibilities.

Master Ra commenced a new sequence, his movements a visual symphony of elegance and strength. The first time was slow, almost meditative, allowing for close observation. But the second repetition had a quicker tempo, like a coiled spring releasing its tension. Ryu found herself mentally mirroring the moves, the imagery of each stance and shift imprinted in her mind. Her eyes darted towards Tom; he synced subtly with the Master as if trying not to showcase his familiarity with the routine. On the next repetition, the entire room moved in unison, their bodies a living, breathing tapestry of synchronicity.

"Close your eyes," Master Ra's voice filled the room, layered with gravitas.

Ryu's eyelids descended like curtains, turning her sight inward. Her heart pounded in her chest, rhythm syncing with her quickened breaths. She felt a wave of apprehension; she had no visual guide but only the internal rhythm and muscle memories that seemed almost preternatural.

Yet, the movements came surprisingly easy. Her arms and legs maneuvered through the invisible air as if guided by some instinctive choreography. In her mind's eye, the silhouette of an assailant took form—she parried an imaginary attack and disarmed him in the dim theater of her imagination.

"And stop," RA's voice broke through, pulling her back to reality. "Relax and open your eyes."

Her eyes flickered open, adjusting to the dim light diffused through the room. Her breaths were deeper now, her heart racing yet steady, and a wave of elation washed over her like a warm embrace.

“That’s enough for this evening,” RA announced, his voice laden with finality. “Time to get some rest.”

The boys began to disperse like leaves carried away by an autumn wind. Ryu moved to join them but halted when Master Ra’s voice sliced through the silence. “Where did you learn to do that?” he questioned, eyes locked onto hers like twin beams of scrutiny.

“I’m sorry,” Ryu stammered, momentarily disoriented. “I haven’t done this before, ever. Tonight was the first time.”

A long, silent pause filled the space between them, RA’s eyes searching hers as if trying to decode an enigma.

“I’d like to run through one more routine,” he finally said, breaking the silence. “I will demonstrate only once. See if you can replicate it.”

“Of course,” Ryu replied, bracing herself for the challenge.

Master Ra’s movements were a blur of precision, his body twisting and swaying like a reed in the wind. The instant he stopped, Ryu moved.

As Ryu began replicating the intricate martial arts routine demonstrated by Master Ra, a transformation began to manifest. Unbeknownst to her, the latent power within her, the Dragon Aura, started to emerge. The aura was a fiery manifestation of her ancient Egyptian kung fu lineage, a power as formidable as mysterious.

As she gracefully moved through the steps of the routine, her body seemed to radiate an otherworldly energy. Her skin took on a subtle, radiant glow, and her movements became more fluid and precise. Her hair, tied back, seemed to come alive, undulating as if moved by an invisible wind. A faint, ethereal light danced around her, casting a warm, fiery hue over her form.

Master Ra watched in awe as this transformation unfolded before his eyes. He could see the fire-like aura surrounding her, a potent symbol of her inherited power and the mastery of her movements. The room seemed to grow warmer as if stirred by the intensity of this newfound energy.

Ryu herself remained unaware of the changes taking place within her. She continued to execute the routine flawlessly, each movement imbued with a fiery grace. The room seemed to pulsate with an ancient power, her mind replaying his complex sequence. Her limbs moved through the air with newfound confidence until she was still in a waiting stance.

When RA finally spoke, his voice was tinged with an unspoken gravity. "I think we need to talk."

THIRTY ONE

Master Ra sat on the plush matting that covered the floor of the dimly lit room, his posture effortlessly erect as he folded his legs cross-legged. The air hung heavy with the earthy aroma of incense, wafting in languid swirls from a brass burner in the room's corner. Ryu took her place across from him, her legs folding with some effort, her eyes locking onto the wise glint in RA's gaze. When he took a deep breath, it was as though he inhaled the very essence of the room; his chest expanded noticeably, and he exhaled with a serene tranquility that seemed to wash over Ryu like a comforting tide.

With that breath, he began to unfurl his tale. His voice, a mellifluous baritone, seemed to dance on the edges of Ryu's consciousness as he spoke of ancient events, forgotten dynasties, and destinies unfulfilled. The intangible became almost tactile as he said, the atmosphere laden with the gravity of his words. Ryu was pulled into the narrative but remained adrift, her mind struggling to tether the profound utterances to some semblance of understanding.

When Master Ra's words finally tapered off, Ryu felt like she had been traversing an enigmatic maze. "And this is why you have a destiny to fulfill," he pronounced, every word imbued with a potent blend of conviction and gravity.

"But..." Ryu's voice quivered as she began, her eyes narrowing in awe and bewilderment. RA raised his hand, its skin etched with the topography of countless life experiences. The room seemed to still be in deference to his unspoken command.

"We have used the word many times, but it is right, now, that you understand what that destiny is," he continued, "but first, there is something else you must know."

A sense of hesitation clouded RA's venerable eyes. Was he deliberating over what to reveal? Ryu wondered if he might even be fabricating an explanation, but that seemed inconceivable given the palpable weight of the atmosphere.

"For a long time," he resumed, "archaeologists were forbidden to excavate in the Valley of the Kings. But permission was recently granted." His eyes sparkled as if imbued with hidden knowledge. "They've unearthed what they believe to be a pyramid complex hidden deep below layers of time-hardened sand. They've also discovered something unsettling—a portion of a single body."

The mere notion struck Ryu like an arrow. "The pharaohs?" she blurted out, skepticism supplanted by a gnawing fascination.

"It is certainly possible," he responded, his voice tinged with an almost otherworldly gravitas.

His following words were grave. "We must never speak his name."

"Why on earth not?" Ryu's incredulity resurfaced, clashing with the enigmatic aura RA had woven.

He sighed, a sound like the rustling of ancient manuscripts. "Call it superstition, if you will. We simply do not."

RA's eyes narrowed. "The body part they found was a hand, and it's eerily well-preserved as if it's been lying there merely years, not millennia."

Ryu's eyes widened. "But that's impossible," she whispered.

RA leaned in closer, the lines on his face deepening with earnestness. "That hand retains a residual energy, an enduring power. It could be cataclysmic or divine, but its potency cannot be questioned. It could be invaluable to those who understand it."

Ryu's initial skepticism was overtaken by a creeping sense of awe. "It's more than just a story, isn't it?"

RA's face was etched with the solemnity of countless generations. "There might be no limit to what whoever gains possession of it could achieve."

As he spoke, the weight of Ryu's nascent destiny pressed upon her with newfound intensity, as tangible and unyielding as the surrounding walls.

"But who would even be aware of it?" The words hung in the air, thickening the dimly lit room's tension. Ryu could almost taste the electricity between them.

"The people who killed Eileen and Jack," Master Ra's voice was like gravel, "because they knew they needed to get hold of it before you do."

Confusion knitted Ryu's brows, making her forehead feel heavy. "But why would I want to get hold of it? I don't understand."

The flickering candlelight danced across Master Ra's weathered face as he spoke, illuminating the deeply etched lines of his years. "Because that's your destiny. To destroy any trace of the Pharaoh—a man doomed to return sooner or later. And I think that time is nearly upon us. But you are not ready yet; you are still far from ready."

Her heartbeat accelerated, a rhythm of unanswered questions

pounding in her chest. “What more do I have to do to be ready? And what happens when I am?”

Master Ra’s eyes became bottomless wells of contemplation, holding the weight of ancient secrets. “You have to stop the leader of those killers, the puppet master behind the scenes. You may be the only one who can. But you will fail if you try too soon and are not ready. And then, there would be no stopping him.”

A shiver snaked down her spine. “But why me? Of all the people in the world, why me?”

The air grew heavy, almost tangible, as Master Ra paused. “Because you have inherited something from your mother that grants you a potential power others can’t even fathom.”

Ryu laughed, a sound that felt jarring in the heavy air. “What, like I’m some kind of Chosen One? Is that the line we’re taking?”

Master Ra’s voice deepened, resonating like a drum. “It’s not about choice; it’s a matter of birth, of lineage. Your ancestor was there the day the Pharaoh was brought down. You’re a very special child, Ryu.”

Doubt and disbelief danced in her eyes, but her laughter stilled. “You’re dead serious, aren’t you?”

His gaze was unyielding, a granite pillar. “I never jest about these matters. Even if you don’t believe me now, I ask you to trust me for the moment.”

She felt her skepticism waver, if only for a heartbeat. “You haven’t said what I must do to be ready. Do I just need to complete your challenges? Will that be proof enough?”

His eyes softened like the first light of dawn breaking the night. “It will go a long way, but even that might not suffice.”

Eager but uneasy, she pressed, "Then we should continue tonight. The sooner I do what needs to be done, the better."

A palpable fatigue settled over him like a shroud. "Not tonight, Ryu. You need to rest. Tomorrow, we begin anew, and you must prepare to dig even deeper."

She felt a flicker of excitement tinged with trepidation. "Starting with another stone?"

A smile twitched at the corners of his lips, so slight it was almost lost. "Starting with another stone."

THIRTY TWO

That night, she dreamt in a swirling haze of darkness and movement, locked in combat with the shadowy figure she had once envisioned while practicing her routines with her eyes clenched shut. This time, he was a force to be reckoned with—muscles rippling under the skin as dark as coal, his movements a liquid blur of lethal intent. Every strike of his echoed like a drum in her ears, reverberating through her bones. Whenever he lunged, she parried, her arms quivering under the strain, sweat making her palms slippery on the hilt of her weapon. She was wilting, a flower under a relentless sun, gasping for breath as if the air had thickened around her. It felt like he was reading her soul, preempting her every move, countering with something faster or smarter. She woke with a start, her skin clammy, the haunting visage of the looming figure imprinted on the insides of her eyelids.

It was still the dead of night, the air thick with the sort of silence that presses on the eardrums. Her roommates were asleep, their rhythmic breathing a whispered counterpoint to the deafening quiet, a soft reminder of their existence, even as emotional distances had started to creep between them.

The rest of the building lay in somnolent stillness when she padded through the kitchen, her feet silent on the cold tile. Stepping out into the pre-dawn chill, the sky above was a gradient of Indigo, promising the light but withholding it still. The path down the hillside was a murky channel of inscrutable darkness, but her body was a live wire, buzzing with untapped energy. She couldn't bear to wait for the dawn. Striding purposefully, she ran, her feet barely skimming the ground, a whispering dance over gravel and earth. Her pulse was a frantic drumbeat in her ears. When she finally stopped at the pile of rocks at the hill's base, her lungs burned with the sweet ache of exertion. She picked up a larger and more unwieldy stone than before, but she ran back as if it were a feather, propelled by a wellspring of newfound energy.

When she deposited the rock outside the temple, the sun was a timid smudge of orange on the horizon. Her eyes widened to see a lamp glowing near the entrance. Curiosity snaked through her veins; she had watched Master Ra extinguish that very lamp last night, plunging the exterior into pitch darkness before she had retreated to her room.

Gently, almost reverently, she eased the temple door ajar, her eyes falling on Master Ra. He was a fluid tapestry of motion, each movement etched with decades of mastery, his eyes obscured by a dark bandana. It was like he danced with invisible demons, an uncanny grace to his every step. She thought she was a mere ghost in this sacred tableau until he froze, his body angling toward the door. "Come in, Ryu," he intoned, the bandana still in place over his eyes.

"How did you know it was me?" she murmured, awe lacing her words.

"Who else would be up at this ungodly hour? Have you returned with your stone already?"

"Yes," she answered.

"You made excellent time," he remarked. "I watched you

depart, although you were unaware of my presence."

She shook her head, momentarily forgetting his obscured vision. "No, I didn't see you. I didn't expect anyone else to be awake."

"That is a flaw you must rectify. Constant awareness of your surroundings is paramount. Anticipate the unexpected; your upcoming task will demand combat skills and stealth. And remember, you may not choose the battleground. The fight could just as easily choose you."

"Are you trying to tell me they could come here?" Ryu's voice quivered, her eyes darting across the dimly lit room, its walls shadowed in the flickering candlelight.

"It is possible," Master Ra's voice was a rich, earthy timbre that filled the chamber, "and you should be prepared for it."

"But how could they even know we're here?" Her eyes were vast pools of incredulity, almost absorbing the scant light.

RA's eyes were like shards of obsidian. "Nothing remains secret forever. Secrets can slither from the shadows, no matter how tightly they're held."

Ryu felt a chill crawl up her spine, a shiver of fear she couldn't suppress. "The young man who brought us here," she murmured, her words almost swallowed by the thick air.

"Marco is a good boy," RA assured, the words punctuated with an almost paternal authority.

"Then why did he lie to you and sneak off like that?"

"Marco has a life beyond this place, responsibilities that weigh on him. He won't betray us," RA's voice resonated like a ritual chant to ward off evil spirits.

Ryu sensed the atmosphere shift, heavy with RA's unspoken

concerns. She couldn't shake off the worry gnawing at her, the insidious fear that Marco might be their undoing.

Finally, Master Ra removed his blindfold with a flourish. The fabric slipped through his gnarled fingers, a waterfall of black silk before he carefully folded it and tucked it into his worn leather belt. "Are you ready to train hard today?" The question snapped the tension, recentering the room's energy.

"I am," Ryu affirmed, her jaw clenched.

RA circled her slowly. "Do you remember the first sequence of moves you learned yesterday?"

"Of course," she snapped to a ready stance, her muscles tingling in anticipation, the air thickening around her as if charged by her focus.

"Show me."

Ryu's limbs exploded into action, her feet gliding over the stone floor as if it were iced. She moved through the pattern, her body a blade cutting through the tense atmosphere, each move more fluid than the last.

"Good, now faster," RA commanded, stepping into her combat zone. She realized with a start that he wasn't mimicking her; he was acting as her imagined assailant, dodging her kicks and punches by a hair's breadth, his movements almost ghostly.

His hand shot towards her shoulder, a claw poised to strike, to off-balance her. Instinctively, Ryu twisted her body, evading his grasp and seizing his outstretched hand. A quick twist, and she felt the tension of his ligaments.

But then doubt seized her. She panicked, releasing her grip. Like a tiger pouncing, RA swept his leg underneath her, and she crashed onto the floor, her body colliding with a resounding thud.

"Why did you stop!" His voice was a roaring thunder, shaking the room.

"I thought..." she stammered, disoriented.

"You thought what? That you had already learned enough to beat me? That I'm some frail old man who knows nothing?" His words cut through her like shards of ice. "Foolish child, you have so much yet to learn. Perhaps too much. I hope I'm not wasting my time with you. Go and get some breakfast. I'll have decided what to do with you when you return."

THIRTY THREE

Ryu's eyes stung, a tempest of emotions swirling within her as she closed the heavy wooden door behind her. Each thud of the closing door reverberated like a drumbeat, echoing the stern words of Master Ra. She clenched her fists, nails digging into her palm, determined not to let him see the impact of his stinging rebuke. A haunting doubt gnawed at her core, but she quashed it, transforming it into a steely resolve.

As she descended the ancient stone steps toward the dining hall, the air grew heavier, almost palpable in its thickness. Why had Master Ra allowed her that fateful attempt? Her thoughts darted to and fro like a moth entrapped in a lantern. Could it have been a test, a riddle wrapped in the guise of a lesson? Her mind tangled with memories of the phantom menace infiltrating her dreams last night—an omen, perhaps.

Reaching the communal space, Ryu settled into her seat, the rough-hewn wooden bench beneath her feeling colder than usual. She hardly spoke, her words mere whispers that skated across the surface of routine courtesies. The other girls eyed her sidelong, their gazes distant and slightly askance. The once-shared camaraderie had fractured; they were diverging onto separate, inscrutable paths.

Ryu rose with the boys, her plate still warm with untouched food. Nobody expected her to help with the chores anymore. A curtain of silence fell between her and Master Ra, each word left unsaid an arrow in a quiver. The boys, aware of the tense atmosphere, headed straight to the chambers of trial, the creaking of the ancient temple door heavy with unspoken challenges.

Finally alone in the dimly lit temple, adorned with shadows and flickering candlelight, Master Ra turned toward her. "You have much to prove, Ryu—both to me and yourself," he intoned, his voice sinking into her like a dagger. "Your training intensifies today. Should you fail, it'll be a glaring sign that my time is squandered on you. Is that understood?"

Summoning the fragments of her pride, Ryu dipped her head. "I understand, Master," she murmured, tasting the bittersweet tang of humility and apprehension.

A guttural grunt escaped him as he swiveled away, leading her through the labyrinthine corridors. The distant clatter and strain of the boys in other chambers punctuated the air—a cacophony of effort and struggle. Yet Ryu's eyes stayed riveted on Master Ra's stoic back, her focus razor-sharp, as though she were threading a needle in the dark.

Upon entering the next chamber, Ryu was met with an abyss of shadowy space, the ceiling almost swallowed by the dark. Ropes dangled ominously from some unfathomable height. The absence of leather bags felt like a foreshadowing of an entirely different breed of challenge.

"Can you climb a rope?" His question felt less like an inquiry and more like an ultimatum.

She nodded, her memories flickering to previous gym classes—each moment on the rope a battle against gravity, her shoulders a canvas of dull ache for days.

His eyes narrowed. "You seem unsure."

Her voice tightened, attempting to shroud her hesitancy. "I can."

"Prove it," he barked, flinging a rope toward her like a gauntlet thrown. "Climb to the top and ring that bell. Or don't bother coming down."

Ryu's fingers curled around the coarse rope, the fibers scratching against her skin. Her gaze lifted toward the void above, where the rope vanished into darkness. With a surge of adrenaline, she leaped upward, seizing the rope. Her technique failed her, her feet slipping, but her arms—fueled by urgency—pulled her higher and higher. She scaled the abyss, each breath a gulp of strained air until finally, her hands found the bell, almost lost in the cavernous dark.

Heart pounding like a war drum, she rang it—a clarion note that pierced the silence, resounding through the chamber and deep within her soul.

She remembered the raw, visceral danger of letting the rope burn through her bare palms, and despite that knowledge, she plummeted down with the force of a diving falcon. When her feet kissed the ground, her eyes locked onto Master Ra's face. His eyes widened just a fraction—a flicker of surprise he couldn't mask. Yet his voice was an impenetrable fortress, giving nothing away.

"The challenge before you is no child's play," he began, his eyes narrowing as if sizing up her soul. "Climb, rope to rope, ringing the brass bell that hangs in the shadowed heights of each. Twelve ropes, twelve bells. A single misstep, a single plummet, and you fail. No net below, no savior in sight. Contemplate well before you nod, Ryu. If you fail, it's likely your swan song in this temple. Do you understand the gravity?"

But she felt no gravity; she felt invincible. "I'm ready," she vowed, each word etched in steel.

His eyes held a new glint. "Then remember every lesson, every scar, every fall you've ever had—you'll need them. Godspeed."

She didn't ponder the weight of his words. Springing off the ground, she grabbed the rope, her hands clamping around it as if it were the lifeline it literally was. Without looking back, she shot upwards, a human arrow, as if the earth had swallowed the abyss below. Once within the gloom of the ceiling, she tapped the brakes, the dark eating her form. Her hand met cold brass; the first bell tolled like a distant storm. One down, eleven to climb.

Her knuckles whitened as she reached for the next rope, swinging toward it like some primordial ape. Her heart stopped as her grip slipped—an inch, a millimeter, a universe in that moment of free-fall. Down below, the Master was a statue, a sphinx in human form, unreadable and silent. With a growl, she pulled herself back up to ring the second bell. The echo hung in the air like a warning.

Each subsequent rope seemed to stretch farther away, like stars in an ever-expanding universe. Her eyes narrowed; her body became an oscillating pendulum, swinging in wider arcs each time, each swing a mounting crescendo in this symphony of tension.

Then, a flash of light from below. Her eyes met Master Ra's—did they glint with hope or a cruel wager? She couldn't tell, but his enigmatic gaze fueled her fire.

Her arms were molten lava, her muscles frayed cables on the verge of snapping. As she reached the twelfth rope, her grip faltered, a half-miss that left her hanging by a thread, a whisper away from defeat. Her shoulder shrieked in agony, a firework of pain bursting in her joint. Her free hand flailed, desperate for a hold, her legs mimicking the chaotic dance of a marionette cut from its strings. The ground below was a yawning maw, ready to swallow her whole, bones and all.

But she clenched her teeth, her resolve unshakable even if her grip wasn't. With a guttural roar, she seized the rope with her other hand, stabilizing her swing like a trapeze artist teetering on oblivion.

For now, she had conquered gravity; she had conquered doubt. And as she rang the final bell, its chime resonated through the chamber like a paean to her indomitable spirit.

It was a precarious height, a distance where any plunge to the earth below would be an agony of shattered bones and extinguished hopes. Yet, Ryu didn't fall. With every sinew screaming in agony, she coiled the rope around her leg, clamping it between her feet in a desperate bid to divert some of the searing strain from her overburdened shoulder. The rope, however, oscillated like a pendulum of doom, adding to the mounting complexity of her predicament.

Her eyes darted, searching for the bell through the ink-black void above her. For a moment, nothing—only an abyss that seemed to gaze back into her soul. And then, like a phantom materializing in the night, she discerned it—a dark mass looming in the heart of the halo of ropes. A sanctuary is so tantalizingly close yet sadistically distant. For a split second, the notion of retracing her route flitted through her mind, but her shoulder's fiery protest snuffed that thought out. Could she even manage a retreat without breaching this torturous test's unstated rules?

Just as she hovered on the brink of decision, Master Ra's voice rose from the cavernous depths, shattering the silence. "You have to sound the bell from that rope."

The words were a lifeline, a single gleam of guidance in an ocean of chaos. In that instant, she sensed that, against all previous evidence, he yearned for her to succeed.

With resolve forged in the crucible of countless failures, she first adjusted her swinging arc. Every sway was a struggle, each swing draining her reserves, heightening the life-or-death tension of her aerial ballet. Yet no matter how hard she lunged, her fingertips fell excruciatingly short. Each failed grasp was a mocking echo in the suffocating silence.

Time was running out; her body screamed for relief. Then, like a lightning bolt, realization struck her—a final, perilous gambit. Her heart pounded in her chest as she tightened her feet around the rope, squeezing as if her life depended on it. Taking a vertiginous breath, she launched the rope into its most extreme arc yet. At the sheer climax, she did the unthinkable—she let go.

Her arm lunged through the air, every muscle fiber stretched taut as a bowstring. Her outreached hand grazed the icy metal just as the bell erupted in a triumphant clangor, reverberating through the hollow chamber like the sweet tolling of destiny fulfilled.

She was unshackled, free, victorious for that brief, exhilarating moment.

And then her world shattered into blackness.

THIRTY FOUR

There was movement in the blackness, shapes that constantly shifted and surged, accompanied by a cacophony of screeching that threatened to drown out the sound of the great bell. It took a moment for her to realize what the mass was: bats, hundreds of them, swarming around her, tangling in her hair as she descended. In her panic, she nearly forgot the lethal danger of falling until the rope snapped taut around her leg, arresting her plummet. Ryu screamed in agony and scrambled to clutch the rope. She almost had it when one foot slipped, sending her sliding down the rope, the abrasive fibers digging into her flesh even through her trousers.

Her free leg flailed, desperate to slow her descent but failing. However, as she emerged into the light, she caught sight of the rope. Now hanging upside-down, she snatched hold of it and pulled it tightly to her. Relief surged through her, but she was still hurtling toward the ground, Master Ra looming ever larger below her. She tightened her grip, the friction searing her bare skin but slowing her descent. Miraculously, she came to a complete halt just a couple of feet from the ground. Unwinding the rope from her leg, she felt immediate relief as blood flowed back into her limbs. Unable to contain herself, she collapsed to the ground, her legs giving way beneath her. Master Ra waited momentarily before extending a hand to help her.

"That was the most difficult of the tasks," he said. "But I hope you understand why I did not allow you to attempt it first."

Ryu hadn't even given it a moment's thought. She had been too preoccupied with staying alive, let alone completing the task.

"I guess you didn't want me dead before I'd tried a few of the others?" she joked grimly.

The nod he gave was as slight as the smile on his lips. "It would be a sad loss to the world if the power inside you was not allowed to reveal itself."

"I wasn't ready," she said.

"That is also true, but the training has improved you beyond all understanding in just a few short days. And your mind is sharper, too."

What training? I've been participating in these challenges unless you discussed the time with the boys last night.

"They have certainly contributed, but there is much more than that."

Ryu was puzzled, but then she remembered the small pile of rocks she had brought up from the bottom of the hillside. On that first morning, she had struggled to climb back up with a stone far smaller than those she had carried since. Today, she'd practically sprinted up with a much heavier rock and had found herself barely winded. Surely people didn't get much fitter with just a few days of exercise?

"What's happening to me?" she asked.

"You are becoming," Master Ra replied.

"Becoming? Becoming what?"

"That remains a tantalizing enigma," he murmured, his eyes almost dancing with inscrutable meaning. "But suffice it to say, all the whispered legends were not mere fables. The seeds have been sown, and perhaps—just perhaps—they're blooming at the precise moment they're needed. Even though you're not yet fully formed."

A maelstrom of questions swirled within Ryu's mind. The enigmatic words tantalized her, inciting frustration and a feverish desire to understand. Just as she was on the cusp of bursting, demanding clarity, the outer door of the temple creaked open with a sense of urgency. A voice trembled through the air, tinged with desperation as it called for Master Ra.

"One...moment," he announced, punctuating the words as if they were filled with an untold weight. "I am called elsewhere."

He turned his back and departed, vanishing into the labyrinthine temple. Ryu was left ensnared in a silence so heavy it was almost palpable. The bats that had swarmed earlier retreated to their dark crevices, shrouding the chamber in a deceptive tranquility that belied the urgency in the voice she had just heard.

Torn between following him and respecting his implied wishes, she hovered at the threshold, immobilized by indecision. Straining her ears, she tried to catch fragmented whispers, but RA had evidently soothed the frantic young messenger; their voices were now, but soft murmurs, unintelligible echoes that left her further unmoored.

Finally, he returned, his face an unreadable mask. Without fully reaching her, he beckoned, his eyes alight with an intense yet somber urgency.

"Quickly now," he intoned. "We mustn't tarry."

"What's happened?" she asked, her voice quivering as she matched her pace to his longer strides, her heart pounding in sync with her footfalls.

"Alas, it involves your sister," he replied, still not facing her, his voice fraught with a complexity she couldn't begin to parse.

"Thalia?" Her voice wavered, threaded with both confusion and a dawning dread. "What mischief has she entangled herself in now?"

He paused, finally turning to lock eyes with her. "No mischief on her part," he said, his voice dipping low, each word like a drop of ice. "They've taken her."

The world teetered, tilting on its axis. All the triumphs, the exhilarating conquest of the rope, the bell, her growing sense of empowerment—each evaporated, leaving a hollow void that seemed to consume her soul. Ryu felt as if she were plummeting anew, only this time, there was no rope to catch her fall.

THIRTY FIVE

"Taken her? Who's taken her?" Ryu's voice quivered with a barely contained panic. The room felt airless as if all the oxygen had been sucked away in the wake of RA's words. Her mentor's silence hung like a guillotine blade—cold, inevitable.

He said nothing more until they arrived at the boys' dormitory. Inside, a sense of trepidation hovered like a dark cloud. Sarah and three boys were circled around a bed as if participating in some macabre vigil. Their faces were etched in lines of worry so deep, they seemed carved.

"You can leave," RA commanded, his voice slicing through the dense atmosphere. The boys scattered, revealing Marco—pale, prone, and battered—on the bed.

"Marco!" Ryu's voice shattered like glass. "Is he..."

"He's hanging by a thread," Sarah cut in, her eyes refusing to meet Ryu's as if the truth might be too harrowing to acknowledge even with a glance.

"What in God's name happened to him? And what—what does this have to do with Thalia?"

RA's face was a mask of grim resolution. "He's been tortured, Ryu. They were extracting a location—a place—from him."

"A place? You mean—"

"Here, Ryu. They wanted to find you."

A silence heavier than stone settled over the room. Ryu's heart pounded, her veins icy with dread. "Then why did they take Thalia?" The answer came to her even as she said the words—a terrible, twisted mirror reflection of her fears. They had mistaken her sister for her.

"We need to get her back," Ryu's words tumbled out, desperate, fragmented.

"That's not your burden to bear," RA's words were ironclad, unyielding.

"They're looking for me. I'll swap places with her, just let me—"

"You're not prepared," RA cut her off, his tone an impenetrable wall.

"Then what will prepare me? More trials? Another—what? Tell me!"

RA's eyes locked onto Ryu's. "You would need to defeat me. Hand-to-hand. Weapons. Your choice."

Ryu's mind swirled in confusion and doubt. Was he serious? But then again, the real issue was impossibly, painfully immediate. Her sister was in peril.

"First, we need to pinpoint where they've taken Thalia. Marco may know," RA finally said, redirecting the focus.

"I can help him," Sarah interjected, "but no interrogation. He's on the edge; he can't take more."

"Why did Marco even leave?" Ryu's voice quivered, grasping at straws, trying to make sense of a world upended.

"He found his mother. He'd go to hell for her," Sarah revealed. "He even had a cell phone here—in case she needed him."

The room felt like it was closing in on Ryu, the walls drawing nearer, suffocating her with layers of unspeakable choices and unimaginable costs. Her sister's life teetered on a razor's edge of time and decisions, each tick of the clock mocking her with its unforgiving march.

RA's voice cut through the air like a blade. "Time is slipping through our fingers. Sarah, do whatever you can for Marco. The enemy will soon realize their mistake and come back. We have no moments to spare." His eyes met Ryu's. "Prepare yourself. You have an hour. Be back at the temple."

As Ryu stepped outside, she felt the atmosphere thicken with tension. The boys, clustered together, were a knot of hushed voices and darting eyes. Words like 'traitor' and 'that girl' pierced the air but fell dead as they noticed her standing there.

"Marco is no traitor," she declared, her voice trembling with anger and desperation. "You think you know torture? He endured the unendurable and didn't give us away!"

The rebuttal from one of the boys was a slap. "None of this would've happened if you hadn't been here." He turned away, leaving her words to evaporate in the charged air.

With a heart pounding like a drumbeat of war, she rushed to find Indigo. She was hunched over on their bed, convulsed in sobs. The sight was like a fist around Ryu's lungs.

"Hey," Ryu's voice barely rose above a whisper, a vain attempt to navigate the field of emotional landmines.

"What do you want?" Indigo's words were barbed, and her grief turned to a sharp edge.

"I need to know you're okay."

"Okay?" Indigo bolted upright, eyes swollen but ablaze. "You've been off playing hero while Thalia and I have been reduced to nothing! Forgotten! You've barely said a word to us!"

Ryu opened her mouth to object but then bit back her words. Now was not the time for excuses. The reality hung like a guillotine: Thalia was in danger, and words would not save her.

"I'll make it right," Ryu choked out, but Indigo shrugged off her attempt at a reconciling touch. Alienated, Ryu left, swallowing her own budding tears.

As she trudged up the path to the temple, she was haunted by the thought that Master Ra was hiding something. If the key to unlocking those secrets lay in passing his cryptic tests, then so be it. She wouldn't—couldn't—linger to check on Marco. Any change in his condition, after enduring tortures she could barely fathom to keep their secrets, would be a change for the worse. And if that grim turn came to pass, she was braced for the torrent of blame she knew would flood her way.

THIRTY SIX

Master Ra was already back in the temple when she reached there, his posture disciplined, his eyes closed—stillness amid palpable tension.

"You're early, Ryu," he intoned, eyes closed.

"Everyone out there seems to be against me, even though my sister was the one taken," she shot back, urgency lacing her words. "I have no time to waste. I have to get her back."

"Even if it costs your own life?"

"Especially if it does. She's all I have. I made her promises."

His eyes flicked open, piercing her soul as if measuring her resolve. Then, he was on his feet in a fluid motion that seemed to defy his years. "If you're so determined, then prove you're ready. Complete the remaining challenges, defeat me in single combat, and I'll arm you with every piece of wisdom I possess."

There was an unspoken challenge there—a test of skill and her very mettle. She could feel it. She needed no one else's life hanging in the balance; she could hardly bear the weight of her sister's peril. "I'll take that challenge," she said, her voice thick with resolve.

"Any lingering pain from the bell challenge?"

She shook her head, almost surprised. "No, I feel ready. More than ever."

"Then let's waste no more time," he said, his voice razor-sharp. "But make no mistake, if you fail today, there will be no do-overs tomorrow."

The first challenge melted away beneath her newfound confidence. She dodged and weaved, letting intuition guide her. And just like that, it was done. RA's solitary nod spoke volumes; it was the gravest compliment he could give.

Now, on to her final test. Buckets and poles were set; the leather bags swayed gently as if taunting her. She gripped her pole tightly and scaled her bucket, every muscle taut with readiness. Across from her, RA stood—his pole tucked under his arm, his gaze an unreadable mask.

This was it. Her heart pounded; her grip tightened. Everything hinged on the next few moments, the air so thick with tension she could almost taste it.

"Are you ready?" RA's voice broke through the silence, laden with an intensity that mirrored her own.

She raised the pole, her grip firm but agile. "I am."

Master Ra's pole sliced through the air with deadly speed, a blur of motion aimed at her face. Every muscle in her body tensed, adrenaline surging as she sidestepped, her pole deflecting his with a savage swat. Wood clashed against wood, sending a jolt of raw energy that reverberated up her arm, threatening to numb her muscles—but she held firm.

With no time to lose, Ryu counterattacked. Her pole whirred back, then shot forward like a striking dragon, low and relentless. The attack was a gamble—aimed at his ankles, it carried enough force to snap bone. But she bet on RA's agility, and he leaped, soaring a couple of feet into the air. It was the opening she needed. With a calculated swiftness, she lowered her pole to mere inches from the ground, toppling the bucket that was Master Ra's only foothold.

He landed gracefully, pole released, and for the first time, his eyes met hers with not just respect but a glint of revelation. He bowed deeply. "Very clever," he acknowledged, his voice filled with genuine admiration. "Studying the Dragon Style from the scrolls in the library, you've shown exceptional dedication. You have one challenge left."

"I'd rather not fight you," Ryu interjected, her voice edged with urgency. "What about a foot race up the hill, carrying one of those stones?"

He chuckled, a rich sound tinged with wisdom. "A sprint up a hill won't prepare you for the battles ahead. We can wait until morning."

"No," she shot back, her eyes locked onto his. "It has to be now. I can't afford hesitation; my sister's life hangs in the balance."

"You sound confident of victory."

"I have to be," she retorted, her voice steely. "Failure isn't an option. The threat isn't distant anymore; it's immediate, it's real. I must get my sister back."

RA nodded, solemn yet inspired. "Then choose your weapon, and we'll gather the others. This is a lesson for all."

"Others?" Ryu questioned, her eyebrows furrowing.

"Your test is also theirs. It's a crucible for growth, for everyone."

"How many have passed your tests?"

"Eleven," he disclosed, a wistful tone entering his voice. "But only one defeated me. A choice of weapon made the difference."

Ryu sensed the weight of his words, the unspoken stories behind them. "Marco?" she ventured.

He nodded, a complex sea of emotions swimming in his gaze. "Yes. Marco."

THIRTY SEVEN

Ryu's heart pounded like war drums as she sat cross-legged on the temple floor, desperately trying to find a point of inner calm amid the storm of emotions that swirled within her. The air in the temple was dense with the scent of incense and worn leather, and every inhalation filled her with a heady blend of peace and anticipation. The stone floor beneath her was cool and contrasted with the fiery determination that blazed within her. Her fingers flexed and unflexed, each movement cutting through the palpable, heavy tension in the air.

Outside, the minutes were crawling towards the fateful hour, an hour that could change the trajectory of her life in ways she couldn't even begin to fathom. Master Ra had said this would be a test of skill and endurance, but Ryu knew it was more than that. It was a battle for her destiny, a claim on her self-worth, and perhaps the only way to claw back the life stolen from her sister. The gravity of what lay ahead filled her with a simmering urgency. Every tick of the clock felt like an echo in the caverns of her soul, reverberating louder and louder until it was a clamoring demand for action.

The temple door creaked open, and in walked a procession of young men, each carrying the weight of their own ambitions, each a disciple of Master Ra. As their sandaled feet padded softly across the stone floor, Ryu felt an unsettling mix of reverence and scrutiny. Clouded with curiosity and doubt, their eyes scanned her as they took their positions along the temple walls. Ryu exhaled, grateful that Indigo hadn't joined them. She didn't need the added emotional weight of a friend's concerned gaze tipping her precarious balance.

The walls, which had stood as mute witnesses to countless trials and tribulations, closed briefly, making the space feel like an arena. Their cold, hard surface was adorned with weapons, their metallic gleam imbued with the spirits of warriors long past. They seemed to be whispering tales of valor and tragedy, their silent voices mingling with the collective breath of the gathering to create a chorus of inescapable intensity.

Master Ra stood at the opposite end, his aura a calming antidote to the brewing tempest within Ryu. His eyes, however, were unreadable pools, leaving her wondering what secrets they hid. Was it wisdom or doubt she saw flickering within their depths? With a bow that sent ripples through the fabric of his robe, he broke the silence.

"The challenge is for unarmed combat. The fight will continue until one contestant cannot proceed or until the adjudicators deem one unfit to defend themselves," he announced, his voice a rich timbre reverberating off the stone walls. "This is not merely a fight; it's a crucible to test the essence of who you are. Would the adjudicators please identify themselves?"

Three older boys separated from the wall, one clutching a small gong and a striker. They nodded gravely before taking their original positions. Every heart in the room seemed to sync with Ryu's, every breath held in collective suspense.

Master Ra positioned himself a calculated distance from Ryu, just far enough to make the space between them a no-man's land of potential energy. His muscles coiled like a spring, a lifetime of discipline and mastery condensed into a moment of razor-sharp focus.

"Contestants, are you ready?" the boy holding the gong inquired, his voice cutting through the charged atmosphere of the ancient, mystical arena like a blade.

Ryu's gaze locked onto Master Ra's, and in that moment, the world around them faded insignificance. They were the only two beings in existence, drawn together in a cosmic dance of combat. A nod passed between them, a silent understanding forged in the crucible of martial excellence.

With a resounding strike, the gong shattered the silence, reverberating through the arena like a call to arms. In response, Master Ra lunged forward, his movement deceptively simple, a strike aimed at Ryu's head. But Ryu was no ordinary fighter. She flowed like water, her body a blur of movement, evading the strike with the grace and precision of a true martial artist.

The attempted attack may not have found its mark, but its intent was clear: the test had begun. Ryu stood poised and unyielding, a tempest of martial prowess ready to be unleashed. The arena crackled with an aura of mysticism, and Ryu was prepared to demonstrate her martial arts abilities in a contest of skill and determination.

THIRTY EIGHT

At night, she ran.

Even after the rest of the group had gone to bed in their dorms, she continued running through the dark forest until near-exhaustion, driving herself on and on until her knees were buckling and she was on the verge of dropping, but she persisted. Her limbs ached, and her lungs burned as she pushed herself beyond the limit, driven by some inner compulsion to keep moving.

And despite only having the pale moonlight filtering down through the thick canopy of trees overhead to guide her, she didn't slip or stumble once, even on the most uncertain and rocky terrain.

She flowed like a ghost between the trees, over fallen logs and moss-covered rocks, surefooted and tireless.

The night forest held no fear for her.

Instead of going downhill for the stones Master Ra laid, she went up, savoring the burn in her muscles as she ran. She wondered if, when all the rocks were carried up the mountainside, he'd have one of them take them all back down again. Probably. There was a lesson in that, too. And everything the old man did was about delivering lessons.

She didn't run just for fitness; she needed to burn off nervous energy, or she'd still go to bed feeling restless and unsettled.

The incline was steep, and her legs blazed from the exertion, but she pressed onward and upward, gritting her teeth against the flaring pain. Sweat dripped down her back as her lungs heaved for air. Still, she continued her relentless pace, compelled by an anxious, frenetic energy that could only be tamed by pushing her body to complete exhaustion and then, somehow, *beyond*. So she ran on, the moon lighting her way through the dark forest, focused only on ascending higher and higher up the mountain.

But that wasn't all that was bothering her.

Master Ra had been pushing her relentlessly since he'd brought her to the retreat, setting her increasingly more complex tasks and what felt like impossible challenges. She couldn't tell if he was determined to improve her skills or break her to prove she wasn't ready to face their enemies.

His intensity left her uneasy.

Did he know something she didn't?

Of course he did, he was RA.

A better question was, did he see some threat looming that he hadn't shared with them?

And she felt sure the answer was yes; why else would he be driving her so hard, day after day, barely giving her a moment to rest?

She trusted the old Master, but his behavior was becoming increasingly out of what she'd come to think of as the ordinary.

Which made her fearful there was something big coming that she wasn't prepared for.

His intensity made her nervous and set her on edge.

She wished he would just speak plainly and tell them what they were up against instead of these games, pushing and testing her repeatedly.

But Master Ra kept his own counsel, as was his way.

She would just have to trust that this rigorous training was for her benefit and hope that when the time came, she would be ready for whatever he was preparing her to face. There was little else she *could* do.

She could feel the tension building as she faced her opponents in the sparring ring of the temple courtyard.

The first time she faced the mob of boys, she was surprised and overwhelmed by their sheer mass. Their weight pinned her down, and a couple of them, smarting from her skillful deflections of their attacks, punched her hard, making sure she understood that she wasn't invincible. She struggled against their hold, straining her muscles as she tried to break free. The boys taunted and jeered as they held her down, their blows raining down relentlessly, battering her bloody. Ryu gritted her teeth, refusing to cry out, determined not to show weakness. This was her first real test, and she would not fail.

Gathering all her strength, she broke their hold and rolled away, narrowly avoiding another blow as a fist slammed down. Quick as a viper, she struck out, landing solid hits that sent two boys reeling back. The others hesitated, realization dawning that she was not so easily beaten. With a fierce cry, she launched herself back into the fray, fists, and feet striking in a blur. This time, when the boys came at her, she was ready.

The next day, Master Ra had them repeat the test, but this time, she was ready. With forceful strikes, she disabled many of the boys, ensuring they wouldn't be able to attack her again so quickly. There would come a day when they would fail. Maybe soon. Maybe even tomorrow. Her skills improved markedly after a single day of intense training, and she was determined to keep getting better, to prove to RA he had made the right choice in accepting her. She would prove her worth to them again and again. That was the promise she made to herself.

By the third day, many boys hobbled from their injuries but persevered through the training. Seeing their determination despite their pain, Master Ra ended the session early.

On the fourth day, she was stronger still. And by the fifth, they could barely hold their own against her. On the sixth day, she knew that she had the measure of them. Ryu had noticed how the young initiates were determined to prove themselves against her and decided to use that against them. They still considered her an outsider, even though she had been with them for weeks and so desperately wanted to be accepted.

So they tried to beat her, one punch and kick at a time.

But Ryu was just as determined to defend herself against their blows.

Their fierce punches landed with brute force.

Even so, she could nimbly deflect them with the defensive techniques Master Ra had drilled into her, taking the impact on her forearms or turning them into glancing blows with almost hypnotic movement, like a dancer.

She could sense the boys' frustrations growing and reveled in it as she continued to dodge their strikes and counter their attacks with swift jabs and sweeps. Though they outnumbered her, Ryu held her own, in no little thanks to the intensive training she received under RA *and* her nocturnal exertions.

But as the sparring session wore on, she noticed that the boys were tiring much quicker than she did.

She could see the sweat pouring down their faces, rivulets stinging their eyes as their punches and kicks became slower and sloppier.

It became more and more noticeable.

The quick and forceful blows they'd thrown earlier lacked power and precision.

Their footwork grew clumsier as their legs grew heavy.

Their blocks came up late and weak.

Ryu knew instinctively that this was her chance to strike.

Use their fatigue against them and gain the upper hand to end the bout.

She centered herself, drawing on the defensive techniques Master Ra had drilled into her, knowing that reflexes were honed to precision through long hours of practice.

She started landing hit after hit.

Her fists snapped out in sharp jabs to their ribs, and her feet swept their legs out from under them.

The boys wheezed and stumbled, struggling to keep their heads up under the constant assault as Ryu pressed her advantage mercilessly.

Her training was for this: learning to outlast and overwhelm her foes when they were at their most vulnerable.

She would prove herself today, she knew, savoring the brutality of the fight. Her knuckles burned from the repeated impacts, but still, she threw more and more punches, watching the bruises flower across the bodies of these boys who had underestimated her from the start.

Well, no more. They would know all about her after this.

As the last boy fell to the ground, she launched a final attack.

Drawing once more on Master Ra's defensive techniques, she adapted, relying upon her own swift reflexes to rain down blows on the fallen boy until his hands came up, begging for mercy. Her punches landed thunderously, snapping his head back as the punch connected.

He crumbled to the ground, wheezing and groaning.

Ryu stood victorious over their battered forms, chest heaving as she panted, her body drenched in sweat. Her fists ached from the impacts, but she felt an incredible sense of accomplishment. She'd proven herself against the entire coterie of RA's boys. Let them mock her in training now, she thought. This victory validated all those long, grueling hours refining her skills. Every shadow bout, every ghost punch thrown and taken. It had been leading up to this. And she had proven herself worthy.

Master Ra approached her, his wizened face crinkling into a proud smile.

He had overseen her training from the very first day. Sensing the dormant potential, he had pushed her harder than any of the boys. Now, his efforts had borne fruit. She was showing him that she was everything he had hoped she could be.

"You have shown great skill and determination, young one," he said, his voice resonating with approval. "Through dedication to your training and patient mastery of our techniques, I am so very proud to tell you that you have earned your place among the ranks of the Dragon Fist, Ryu, as I always knew you would. You will become a force to be reckoned with, mark my words."

She returned his smile, exhaling in relief as a sense of

accomplishment washed over her exhausted body. After weeks of grueling sessions honing her reflexes, fortifying her fists, and enduring mockery and doubt from the boys she was fighting against to earn her place within their number, she had finally proven herself as good as any of them. Better than most. She had shown them that a girl could stand against any number of boys in combat and emerge victorious. There was a humbling lesson for them.

She was ready now to face whatever challenges lay ahead of her. She was humble enough to understand that her journey was only beginning. Still, this victory had given her the confidence to step forward into her destiny, fist raised, eyes blazing with determination.

That was how she found herself atop the tall mountain behind the monastery, looking out at the distant green valley far below. The exertion of the steep climb had helped clear her mind after the intense training days. She sat down on a large rock to rest her aching legs and contemplate her path forward. Though she had proven herself against the other students over the past few days, she was not arrogant enough to think she had won more than about; more significant trials and tests awaited her.

But at that moment, there was a joy to be taken from the sweeping countryside view from the summit. It filled her with hope and optimism.

She was *exactly* where she needed to be.

Ryu pushed herself to her feet, unthinking, and spun on her heels, ready to fight whatever foe had been foolish enough to sneak up behind her.

Her muscles tensed, and her fists clenched as she turned,

prepared for the attack. Though she could not yet see her opponent, instinct and training-honed reflexes and senses meant they wouldn't get the gift of surprise from her.

She listened intently for any movement or breathing, her eyes scanning the surrounding woods for signs of danger.

Adrenaline coursed through her veins, making her hyperaware and battle-ready.

She would not be caught off guard.

Steadying her breath, she turned slowly in a circle, poised to strike when her unseen enemy was revealed. Whoever they were, she was prepared to defend herself with all her skill. They would be lucky if she let them leave the mountain alive.

"You must be more aware of your surroundings," Master Ra said, his wooden staff ready if she recklessly struck out. She stopped before testing it and potentially facing his swift retaliation, shaking her head and letting out that deep, tension-filled breath.

He was right to chastise her lack of vigilance.

She'd let her guard down in her eagerness to confront her unseen opponent.

Though her reflexes were quick, she'd focused too narrowly on offense rather than being fully aware of potential threats around her.

She bowed her head and waited silently for Master Ra's guidance, resolving to learn from this lesson in situational awareness.

"You have amply demonstrated the natural fighting ability I knew you possessed, child, and perhaps are nearly ready for the trials ahead, but you still have far to go to reach your full potential. I say this for your own good. It gives me no pleasure," he lectured. Though eager to complete her training, she knew he would only deem her ready once he was certain that she had thoroughly mastered both the physical and mental disciplines required in the world outside their temple.

"What more can I do to prove myself?" She asked earnestly, trying to keep the frustration out of her voice. "What final test will show I am ready for whatever comes next?" She met his piercing gaze steadily, willing him to see the determination in her eyes.

"Come with me, I have something important to show you that will help explain," he replied cryptically.

She nodded and followed him silently down from the mountain, curiosity mingling with apprehension about what he intended to reveal.

THIRTY NINE

Master Ra led her back down the hillside to the temple. There were still lamps burning with a warm yellow light in the yard. Their flames flickered gently in the night breeze. She had yet to learn what else there might be for her to see here, given that she knew it like the back of her hand; there was not so much to the ancient temple, the dormitories, standard rooms, kitchens, and the practice grounds. Surely it could not be hiding more secrets?

She was wrong. Very wrong.

As they entered the temple, Master Ra led her past the main chamber, walking towards a corridor towards his quarters, but he had no intention of entering those rooms. He stopped before an area of the wall with a glorious painting of a dragon depicted in lush reds and golds and pressed his fingertips to the great wyrm's glowing eyes. The wall responded to his touch, eliciting a soft snick of a lock being released, and then the wall itself shifted, revealing a hidden door, beyond which lay a winding stone staircase that descended deep into the earth. He led her down the never-ending tight spiral, the air growing cooler and damper as they went deeper.

The stairs opened into an underground chamber, lit by more flickering lamps, though these appeared to be naked flames that never burned out. Strange carvings and artifacts filled the room, the likes of which she had never seen. Ryu gasped in awe at the sight of them, stunned by their presence as much as their beauty. How many more secrets did the temple have to offer up?

Master Ra led her through the vast chamber into a warren of tunnels that ended in doorways. There must have been a dozen of them. Each was marked with some strange symbol she could not decipher. Her imagination ran wild without knowing what lay behind them. "These are sacred chambers," he explained, sensing her curiosity. "Behind each, challenges are laid out that must be mastered if you are to progress with your training, each doorway leading to a challenge significantly more difficult and dangerous than the last. Every acolyte here must take the tests of faith, but few make it to the last door."

She nodded.

"The doors lead to trials designed to test devotion, skill, strength, and ultimately, the soul."

He reached a blank, seamless stretch of stone wall, paused, and turned to her. He had carried a lantern from the warren of tunnels and doors and lifted it to cast a yellow glow over his wrinkled face.

"It is imperative that what I am about to show you remains a secret," he said, his voice low and serious. "Do you understand? Only a handful of my most trusted know what lies beyond this wall."

She nodded earnestly and pledged, "I swear."

He placed the palm of his free hand on the stone and pushed.

A section of the wall slid back soundlessly, revealing a dark opening.

A chill, damp air spilled out as soon as the way opened.

Ryu stared in wonder as yet more secrets were revealed, and understanding that, no matter how many the old man showed to her, there were many more he wasn't. This was more than just a temple; she was in no doubt now.

What confused her was that he didn't seem to have pressed a particular place. There had been no hesitation, no feeling around for the right stone to trigger it, and yet there were no markings like the Dragon's eyes to guide his hand. Curious. A doorway swung inwards; the perfectly cut edges had been invisible in the wall a heartbeat before, and beyond it was a brilliant light that illuminated the way deeper into the temple's depths, ever closer to its true heart.

It took her a moment to realize what was wrong or, instead, what was worse than the existence of the hidden doorway itself. Unlike the eternal flames of the chamber behind them, this was electric light, bright and harsh compared to the flickering torches that lit the rest of the temple.

The air was filled with the gentle but unmistakable hum of banks of electronic equipment.

Master Ra stepped aside and allowed her to go inside ahead of him, "After you, my dear."

She walked through the doorway, her eyes struggling to adjust to the sudden brightness. It was with a growing sense of awe and vertiginous unease that she looked out at the scene laid out below her.

They stood at the top of a metal stairway, the cold, smooth surface feeling unfamiliar under her sandaled feet. But below them - a long way below - was an array of computers and banks of screens, sensors, and other electronic equipment, all lit up with rapidly blinking lights. The soft hum of cooling fans filled the cavernous space. She couldn't begin to imagine the sheer computational power of this place. It was more than any artificial intelligence could ever have needed. More, by far, than a simple martial arts temple run by a preacher with a big heart could ever have needed.

"I don't understand," she said, shaking her head in disbelief.

Those were the only words she could muster in the face of this Batcave… and that was how her brain processed it. There was so much here, the machines gathering information from across the globe, monitoring events, looking for patterns, studying the world as it unfurled, in search of… what? What was RA looking for? Because there was no way he needed this kind of tech array if he wasn't doing something *serious*. And, until a moment ago, she had thought of him as the humble soul who ran a soup kitchen to help the homeless. She stood there, shaking her head, trying to take it all in.

"This is the true heartbeat of our church," he said, his voice echoing off the metal walls. "We are spread far and wide across this world, including the old country. We secretly watch and wait, gathering information to fuel our fight."

Ryu licked her lips, shaking her head. "This must have cost… a small fortune."

"Not so small," he grinned. "A tropical island lair would have cost less… excavating the mountain was no small task…"

"I just… where did all the money come from? Are you a secret billionaire? Do you play poker with Elon or something?" She asked, waving her hand at the mass of advanced technology that seemed so out of place beneath the austere simplicity of the temple up above.

"Would it help you if I told you that came from old wealth? That my family has long since been what you would call rich, so rich the word itself loses all meaning? Or would it be easier to believe that there are generous people out there who have come through the temple doors and others like it? Lost people found themselves at some of our outreach programs, like the soup kitchen. People who needed help, youngsters who needed a leg up and a purpose in life. They receive help and, in time, find themselves in a position to give back; we ask for nothing, but they want to make a difference. Because that could be the truth, too. Or perhaps the money is far older than that and is the result of temple tithes dating back centuries, managed now with all the tools of the modern world to maximize the wealth?" he explained, his voice steady and calm.

"No, not really," she admitted, because truth be told, it didn't matter where the money came from, did it? How it was used made a difference, and RA chose to use it for good, funding his outreach, soup kitchens, and temple. And this place. The server farm that filled a part of this underground facility must have cost tens of thousands of dollars, hundreds of thousands… Maybe even more, she realized. It had to be a match for some of the enormous facilities that housed cloud storage facilities - that themselves consumed more electricity in a day than the rest of the city around them…

She didn't even know what this stuff did, but that didn't negate understanding it was akin to a military base's set-up, and the Army took most of the nation's budget every year.

And somehow, this whole tech bunker had been kept secret.

It didn't escape her noticing that nothing else on the mountain had power. The old man was playing an interesting game, keeping his secrets.

"There's more to see," Master Ra mischievously said, leading the way down the metal staircase to lower levels.

She followed, still trying to work out what might be down here.

She spotted two computer screens—as large as cinema screens—but couldn't make sense of whatever they were displaying, the mysterious symbols and diagrams flashing across the screens too fast to follow.

She slowed to get a better look, but Master Ra moved faster, and she didn't want to lose him as he disappeared through another doorway.

The next room seemed empty except for a soft glow of blue light, though its source was not immediately apparent.

Master Ra closed the door when they were both inside.

The ambient light dimmed perceptibly.

She waited in silence, surprised at how effectively they were cut off from the hum of the server farm and the other electronics. There was nothing to hear in this place, only the rhythmic dub-dub of her heartbeat echoing in her ears.

But then the room was suddenly filled with an ear-splitting roar that shredded through every nerve and fiber of her being and made her ears ache.

She clapped her hands over them in shock, the sound so deafening her knees threatened to buckle beneath her.

A blinding flash of light quickly followed the loud sound, so intense it was akin to gazing into the heart of an eclipse and a deep rumble that made the entire ground shake beneath her feet.

An overwhelming smell of sulfur assaulted her nostrils.

The rumble increased as the room shifted and shivered, trembling around her. Then, a huge masonry slab collapsed, and more debris crashed around her. The cacophony was terrifying. She didn't dare move as more of the ceiling came down. Dust billowed everywhere, and again, the floor bucked under her feet.

Ryu crouched down, making herself small and shielding herself as best she could from the falling rubble hitting the ground around her.

"Master!" she cried out, struggling to make herself heard above the thundering sounds of collapse. It took every ounce of strength she possessed to maintain her balance on the bucking floor without being buried beneath more of the collapse. Her mind shrieked with terror at the idea of the mountain coming down around her; no one would know she was down here or come looking or trying to dig them out. She was going to be buried alive. Another roar echoed in her ears. She shouted desperately once again, willing the old man to hear and somehow know another hidden way out of this coffin before there was no air left for her to breathe…

Her first thought was that this was the Big One, the quake that would tear the entire Western Seaboard apart and leave an entirely new coastline for them to rebuild if they survived… which was not guaranteed with the mountain collapsing in on itself around her.

She had to find Master Ra and get out before they were both buried under the ancient temple.

"Master!" she cried out again, panic rising within her.

There was no reply from the old man, only the continued

rumbling and cracking of stone.

It struck her then: she was alone.

It wasn't that he'd left her willingly; something had taken him from her… a massive boulder to the skull? It was whether he was unconscious or dead…

The light that had blinded her grew brighter still, which was impossible, surely? She had no idea what arcane forces were behind its intense glow; all she knew was that it couldn't be natural… unless the earth's core had somehow broken through the mantle, and she was staring into the heart of the planet…

It filled one entire wall, like a portal to another realm, and with it came such incredible heat, so unbearable she was forced to retreat, shielding her face.

"Master!" she shouted desperately over the deafening din, praying he would miraculously appear, and together they might somehow escape this catastrophe.

Still nothing.

Ryu didn't even know if her voice could be heard above the roaring cacophony of the collapse, only that it was growing louder all the time. The unnatural light and sulfur emanating from the portal intensified, filling the entire chamber with its blinding radiance and rancid reek.

And then, from within it, a monstrous shape began to form in the heart of its fiery heat.

A shape that could not be real.

Could never have been accurate.

It defied everything she knew about the history of the world.

Because it couldn't ever have been real. Not for a single

moment throughout all of history, from the days before mankind, from the days before myth.

And yet…

Her heart hammered. She tasted the copper of blood and fear in her mouth as she gazed upon the form of a great dragon, easily thirty feet long, spouting fire and fury from its fanged maw.

The heat from its breath washed over Ryu, though it did not burn her.

She couldn't move.

The great wyrm moved towards her, scales glistening, shimmering, curls of smoke leaking from its vast mouth. The creature wasn't a dinosaur-like lizard but rather a Chinese dragon with dripping mustaches around the corners of its mouth. She had no idea what they were called.

She knew she should run; there was no way she, a young apprentice, could fight a creature so ancient and powerful.

But something deep inside called to her.

It was as though her blood was responding to its presence.

Like they were kin.

She shook her head.

She couldn't think.

But something about the majesty of that impossible creature convinced her it was not an enemy, or at least that it could not hurt her here in this place - because if it had wanted to, she would be dead already.

No…

This majestic wyrm was a friend, not a fiend.

She licked at the corners of her mouth. Her entire body was

trembling as fear coursed through her, but she wasn't about to run. Not while Master Ra was trapped in there somewhere. To abandon him was cowardice, and after everything she had been through, the one thing Ryu knew about herself above all else was that she was no coward.

She tried to think.

He had disappeared through the temple door just before the portal opened and might be in danger.

The Dragon did not advance, merely releasing flame gouts that filled the chamber. Smoke curled around Ryu. She stood her ground, refusing to so much as flinch. Though the flames burned brightly, she realized they didn't scorch as before. Was that her skin toughening them, or was the creature somehow shielding her from the worst of its heat because it recognized her as kin?

She edged closer to the wall; the narrow door hidden within it had closed behind Master Ra, but it was still there, waiting for her hand to open it. She called his name again over the loud din and moved to the wall. She was sure her voice rang louder this time than the Dragon's deep, rumbling growl. More masonry and rock foundation broke free and came crashing down, so close she felt the rush against her skin as she leaped back.

She had to find her master before there was no way out of the collapsing temple for them.

Still nothing.

Where had the Dragon come from?

What was this monstrous creature that now filled the temple chamber? She kept calling a dragon because surely there could be no… not any real… dragons?

It made no sense.

She had no idea how she could fight whatever name the thing owned.

Nothing RA had taught prepared her to face a mythical creature with her bare hands.

It was too much to hope that Master Ra might have an answer.

She ran, nimbly shifting her direction as the Dragon released another gout of flame, feeling the searing heat pass just a little too close for comfort. Somehow, she slipped past the snarling jaws of the Dragon and slammed her hand against the wall section that had opened up for Master Ra.

Nothing happened.

The bottom fell out of her world at that moment.

The wall remained firmly closed, denying her escape no matter how hard she pounded against the bare stone.

She buckled, broken.

But then her head came up again.

No. Not broken. Only bowed.

She had to find another way to get to RA before the ancient temple collapsed around them under the onslaught of the raging Dragon.

She called his name again as the beast turned to face her, its bulk shifting slowly.

There was no escaping it unless the wall somehow opened.

She ducked low, charging towards it, hands out like claws before her, as its head turned fully towards her.

She reached for one of its thick, scaly legs and leaped up to grab hold of its rough, scaled flesh, but even before she was halfway up its body, the beast disappeared.

She fell to the ground and, on her knees, looked up at the space where it had been, gasping in surprise. Chest heaving, she forced herself to her feet and stumbled forward, standing where the massive creature had been barely a few seconds before, not understanding. The searing heat from its fiery breath was instantly replaced by cool, dusty air.

She frantically felt along the smooth stone wall, searching for any sign of a hidden passage, anything that might trigger a door to be revealed, but found nothing.

The Dragon had vanished as if it had never existed.

FORTY

Her mind could not grasp what had happened.

It reeled, struggling to hold itself together.

But she refused to buckle.

Ryu had seen the creature, whatever it was.

She had felt the heat of the fire that it breathed.

And yet, her brain kept insisting there was no damage to the room, despite having witnessed the ceiling coming down and that massive section of wall collapse to reveal the beast itself.

She stood there, shaking her head.

It defied rational explanation.

Unless it had never been there, despite everything she had seen.

There was something in those thoughts, some clue or realization, that slowly began to come together, but for now, it was just out of reach, fighting against the pounding still filling her ears.

Before her, the concealed doorway within the blank wall opened again, and RA stepped through, a grin on his wizened old face. He did not look like a man in fear for his life.

A moment later, the space filled with harsh electric light, and the truth was revealed.

Ryu stood there, feeling stupid and not a little angry.

There had been no beast, fire-breathing Dragon, collapse, or a massive earthquake.

None of it had been real.

It had all been an illusion — just smoke, mirrors, and light conjured somehow by RA.

She needed help understanding the how or the why.

"How?" she asked, her voice trembling slightly as the adrenaline coursed through her veins. It was as coherent a question as she could manage at that moment, still reeling from the sheer power of the illusion and the fear that had been so real.

"Movie magic, my dear," he said with a sly smile. "It pays to know the right people in this world, and as I say, people come through our doors needing our help at the right time to make a difference… in this case, two brothers with considerable skills in the visual effects world. That Dragon may have only been 'smoke and mirrors,' but it looked real enough to fool you, did it not?"

She nodded. Grudgingly.

"But why?"

"I needed to know how you would react under pressure, and now I know," he explained patiently.

"You did that to me to see if I would break?"

"I needed to see if you would stay and fight or if your first instinct would be to flee. Then there was the question of if you would try to save me during the cave-in, thinking I was in mortal danger, or if you would look to save yourself."

"I hope I passed, then," she said bitterly.

He nodded solemnly. "With flying colors," he said, missing the irony in her tone. "If you had tried to flee to save yourself, I would have known that you were not the one we have been waiting for, no matter how skilled you are. I apologize for putting you through this, but I needed to be certain you had something special inside you — the selfless courage and determination of a true hero."

"But," she was struggling to wrap her head around the sheer cost of all of this and the difficulty of arranging it just for this… "You did it all for this moment? To test me?"

"Ah, dear heart, believe me when I say money is not a problem, it is merely a means to an end," RA replied. "We pay it forward to the next generation and the next when I am gone. Who knows, perhaps they will look to you as Mistress Ryu one day?"

"Wouldn't that be something," she said, offering him a wry grin. "What about the boys studying with you…?" she asked. "Have they been in here? Do they get to face this test too?"

Master Ra shook his head. "As I said, this should not be discussed with the others. They do not know the full extent of our resources, and it is best it stays that way for now… when they are ready, then it will be open to them as it is open to you."

Something about that didn't sit well with her, given that they were up there, performing backbreaking work and barely scavenging enough food for the table when there was the money to live in luxury. "Have you ever wondered how the others might react when they learn the truth?"

"There is no shame in a life of deprivation, child. It builds spirit and character. We are formed in the crucible of experience, and the softer our lives weaken our tempering. We are making souls of steel here. That is my promise to everyone who comes to learn at my temple." She nodded, but still… "What you must consider, of course, is that only those few individuals who succeed with each of the challenges set them will ever get the chance to see this, and to have made it that far, it is sure they are not the ones who would be likely to react adversely. Otherwise, they would have stumbled and fallen at other challenges along the way," Master Ra replied firmly. "I see you doubt my words, but that is all right. I have been working with seekers for a long time and have learned that the boys must learn patience and perseverance before the truth."

"I am curious, Master. Now that I have passed this test? What happens now? What fresh challenge awaits me?" Ryu asked eagerly, glancing around at the ornate treasure-filled cavern.

"You surmise rightly that you still have a lot to learn, dear girl," Master Ra nodded approvingly, "And yes, there is no doubt that you possess an abundance of courage, which this has proven beyond any doubt. Without that, there would be no point in taking your training further."

Again, she nodded. She had known this couldn't be the end of his teaching because, as much of his wisdom as she had taken in, she was sure she had barely scratched the surface. "Am I ready," she said, believing that she was.

And so, a new phase of her training began, more intense and demanding than any she had faced in her first weeks at the temple.

For hours on end, she fought against unreal opponents, as wraithlike as ghosts, that seemed capable of moving in directions that ought to have been impossible for any normal musculature, and perhaps they were. She came down to this chamber to face ancient dragons and winged serpents, to confront huge grizzly bears and venomous snakes, each bigger and faster than anything she could have hoped to meet and survive in reality. More than once, the illusory beasts swiped massive claws. They writhed around her, rending her flesh with such authenticity she could feel the momentary sting and slice, the burn of venom in her veins, every tooth, every claw, but she stood her ground and it passed, fading to nothing as the illusion moved on to the next phase; but so convincing was it, more than once, she screamed and cried out as a blow should have eviscerated her, leaving her guts to spill out across the practice mats.

Her skills were honed in those caverns as she slashed and spun, parried and dodged. Exhausted but determined, she persevered.

After weeks of grueling training against increasingly predatory, illusory foes, Ryu was strapped into a harness and raised on a wire, suspended from a ceiling far above her in the cavernous training hall.

At first, she didn't understand, and then she heard the distant sound of wings and grasped this new development, bracing herself as best she could for the confrontation to come, as those wingbeats turned into the rhythm drumming of a predator coming to rip her into pieces.

She saw it then; its sheer immensity of the mythical beast's immense bulk, impossibly airborne, coming at her, talons extended, ready to rend and rip like her flesh was nothing.

Then they came together, and the battle joined.

And it was everything she had ever feared, but more, it was everything she had ever relished, as she rose to the occasion, surrendering to a base instinct she had never known, as though, somehow, she had unlocked her true self.

For hours, Ryu fought against beasts on the wings, giant birds of prey, and mythical creatures with wingspans more expansive than she was tall, more comprehensive in some instances. The confines of the hall couldn't contain them, and the illusion was so perfect she saw bricks and mortar crumble, stones dislodged by the slice of iron wings, as they came at her.

It didn't matter that she knew none were real; something had changed inside her. Her essence faced each challenge as though they were some repressed memory buried deep in her hindbrain, remembering that once these things were real, she had faced them then and would face them again. For that reason, she could not allow herself to give anything other than her absolute best, giving everything she had to offer, and when she was spent, digging deeper to find more, demand more, drive herself further, harder, faster, punishing her flesh, because when the fight was real, those cuts would do more than sting.

More than once, after a failed attack, Ryu found herself plummeting towards the hard stone ground far below as if the wire had suddenly been cut.

The unforgiving ground rushed up towards her as her body spun out of control, and it seemed impossible that she could stop before crashing, bone-breakingly hard, into it. Yet, somehow, at the very last moment, she was spared the impact and jerked back upwards by the wire, narrowly avoiding what would undoubtedly have been death or grievous injury from such a fall. It was a humbling lesson that as good as she got, her enemies were always just a little better than her. As RA said, such was the world, and it would keep her honest. He had quite the way with words at times.

She convinced herself this grueling training would never end, that Master Ra would always conjure some fresh supernatural challenge to face her, until, at last, he came into the chamber, bowed his head solemnly, then looked up to meet her gaze with fierce pride in his eyes.

"It's time."

She knew the moment she had been working towards had finally arrived, but she was on her knees, having sparred for hours already, exhausting her mind as thoroughly as her flesh and bones.

"Now?" She had not meant to question his wisdom but was so tired.

He nodded.

"The enemy will not wait for you to rest," RA reminded her.

Though exhausted, her skills were honed razor-sharp from the relentless training of these past months as she'd slashed and spun, parried, and dodged; she felt ready.

Breathing hard, chest heaving, she followed him, ready to face whatever RA would throw at her next.

FORTY ONE

The atmosphere in the room was like electricity on the skin, buzzing with a tension that not even a knife could cut through. Master Ra, his knee bandaged tightly, limped his way into the chamber. The strain of the injury was etched across his face, revealing lines that his years of mastery had often hidden. Ryu sensed the weight of his eyes on her. The same eyes that were mirrors to wisdom were now clouded with an urgency that mirrored her own. His gaze shifted towards Marco, lying on the bed, his pallor ashen, and his eyes mere slits.

"You've come," Marco rasped, each word coming out as a laborious effort. Once animated and full of life, his eyes looked sunken, their light dimmed. Bruises painted his face in patches of purple and black, stark against the whiteness of the bed sheets. A thick bandage was wrapped around his forehead, and his arm was in a sling, a manifestation of the physical agony he had endured.

Sarah, her face flushed and eyes red-rimmed, stood near the wall. The distance she put between herself and the bed screamed volumes. She bit her trembling lip, her eyes awash with relief and sorrow. The room smelled of antiseptics, mingling with human sweat and fear. The air felt almost too heavy to breathe.

"Do you know where they've taken her?" Ryu asked, her voice hardly more than a whisper but laden with a dread she couldn't hide. Every tick of the clock seemed to reverberate in the room, each second stretching into an eternity.

A series of coughs escaped Marco, his whole body trembling

like a leaf caught in a storm before he managed to nod ever so slightly. His gaze met Ryu's, and it felt like a jolt of electricity passed between them. The room seemed to shrink, the walls closing in.

"The warehouse," he said, his voice so frail it could break. "The soup kitchen."

The words hit Ryu like bricks, each syllable sending shockwaves through her nervous system. "The soup kitchen? Why?"

"Waiting for someone to return," he added, gasping for air after each word.

Sarah interrupted, her voice filled with urgency. "That's enough. He can't speak anymore; he needs to rest."

Ryu felt as if she were being pulled in a hundred different directions. Her mind was a whirlpool of conflicting emotions—concern for Marco, the desperate need for more information, and a rising fire of determination.

Sarah practically pushed her out of the room, her eyes signaling that the conversation was over. As the door closed behind her, Ryu's ears filled with the loud silence after a storm.

Then, Master Ra was beside her, his face etched with deep lines of concern and physical and emotional pain. His wounded knee seemed to be a burning reminder of the responsibility now thrust upon Ryu's shoulders, a responsibility she couldn't evade. Her pulse was a relentless drumbeat in her ears as if counting down to something—something she couldn't afford to face unprepared.

"They were at the soup kitchen, waiting for someone to

return. If they find out they have the wrong girl, they might still be there," Ryu said, her voice tinged with a newfound resolve.

"But why the soup kitchen?" Master Ra's eyes bore into hers, searching for something only he understood.

"I can't be sure," she answered, "but I can't afford to wait. I need to go now."

Master Ra looked as if he were about to say something, but then his eyes caught something over Ryu's shoulder. Indigo, her eyes still raw but unwavering, gave a slight nod.

"Then go," he said, "and may your path be clear."

Ryu's eyes met his one last time—no longer the eyes of a student looking at her master but those of a warrior acknowledging another. The tension in the room reached its peak and then broke like a wave crashing against the shore, dispersing into a million droplets, each carrying a piece of the burden that had been shared and now lifted.

Without another word, Ryu turned and left, every step echoing the reality she was walking towards—a reality where she could either save a life or lose one. The world's weight on her shoulders felt slightly lighter as she moved, but what was to come felt as heavy as ever.

The tension in the room was palpable, almost like the heavy air before a storm breaks. Indigo's eyes were like embers, smoldering with a fierce light. Ryu could see the muscles in Master Ra's jaw clench as if the room was holding its breath.

"I'm coming too," Indigo's words cut through the air like a knife, her voice unwavering.

"No," Ryu and Master Ra said, almost in eerie unison. It was a rare agreement between the two, a united front that should have been invincible. But Indigo was unmoved.

"You have nothing to offer in this fight," Master Ra continued, his voice laden with an uncharacteristic sharpness. "You will only get in the way and endanger yourself and others."

Indigo's eyes flicked from Ryu to Master Ra and back to Ryu again. A moment of calculation, a split second to gauge whether this was a battle she could win.

"Don't you dare," she seethed, her voice lower but teeming with pent-up fury. "Don't you dare tell me I have nothing to offer?"

Master Ra's eyes narrowed, but it was Ryu who spoke. "Indigo, we can't risk it. This isn't a game. People are in danger, Talia is in danger."

Indigo's lips quivered as she sought to control her emotions, but her voice was resolute when she finally spoke. "I was there, Ryu. I was there when Jack and Eileen were murdered. I've been with you from the very beginning of this nightmare, and you think I'm going to sit here while you go off and risk your life? You think I'll be content being kept in the dark again?"

Ryu bit her lip. She wanted to retort, to argue that it was different this time, but she knew in her gut that it wouldn't be fair. Indigo had been there. She had felt the pain, the loss, just as acutely as Ryu had.

"That's different, Indigo. We were kids then; we didn't have a choice. But now, I can't bear the thought of putting you in harm's way," Ryu said, her voice tinged with desperation.

Indigo stepped closer, her eyes searching Ryu's as if imploring her to understand. "And I can't bear the thought of you going into this alone. If you think I will stay here while my best friend goes off to face God knows what, you're wrong."

Ryu felt a lump form in her throat. She looked at Master Ra, as if seeking an answer, some wisdom to resolve this impossible situation.

Master Ra sighed deeply, the weight of years and responsibilities settling on his shoulders. "Indigo," he began, his voice softer now, almost fatherly, "I understand your sentiments. The courage you're displaying is admirable. But courage without wisdom can be foolhardy."

"Then let me be a fool," Indigo shot back. "Let me be the cheerleader on the sidelines going 'rah-rah Ryu,' if that's all you think I'm good for. But I will be there at the end, no matter what. This pair… they are more than my friends… they are all I have in the world, and if there's a chance, no matter how slim, that I might make a difference… I'm not going to let my *sister* down."

Ryu felt her eyes moisten. She looked at Master Ra again, but it was a plea this time. A plea to let her best friend be by her side, even if it was reckless or dangerous. Because some battles, she realized, were just too monumental to face alone.

Master Ra seemed to consider this, his eyes meeting each of theirs. He was wrestling with his fears and sense of duty to keep them safe. Finally, he spoke, "Indigo, if you go, you will listen to every command either of us gives without question. Do you understand? To do otherwise could be the death of your sisters, and I cannot be worrying about you."

Indigo nodded fiercely, her eyes blazing with triumph and relief.

"Then gather your things," Master Ra said, resignation tinting his voice. "We leave in five minutes."

As Ryu and Indigo exchanged glances, a silent pact was forged between them—an alliance of friendship, of facing whatever darkness lay ahead together. And for the first time in what felt like forever, Ryu felt a tiny glimmer of hope ignite within her.

As they scrambled to prepare in the following minutes, there was an unspoken agreement that they were venturing into the unknown, where the line between bravery and foolishness was perilously thin. But for Indigo, there was never a question; she had been there initially, and nothing would keep her from being there at the end.

FORTY TWO

Big Tito turned out to be a tiny Mexican man who seemed barely large enough to reach the pedals of the battered, old former school bus that waited for them at the bottom of the hill. Ryu pondered how they'd all fit into a single vehicle as they descended. The sight of the bus answered her question.

The bus sputtered, coughed, and rumbled its way toward the city. Ryu noticed that all of the boys had joined them. While she appreciated their company, she also felt a pang of regret that they risked their lives for her sake. Every so often, her eyes met Indigo's; her best friend's eyes were filled with worry and determination.

As for Ryu herself, she glared at a couple of boys who seemed like they might choose to sit beside her, successfully dissuading them. She wanted to be alone with her thoughts. Master Ra was in the front, engaged in casual banter with Big Tito as if this was a typical school outing, not a dangerous mission.

The journey felt interminable, even longer than the ride they had taken in Marco's small car. Silence blanketed them like a heavy cloud. The occasional murmur of small talk among the boys and Big Tito's conversational updates to Master Ra were nothing more than background noise to Ryu. Her thoughts circled Talia, wondering what horrors she might be enduring.

Indigo leaned closer to Ryu, her voice a low whisper. "You know, the last time I was on a school bus, it didn't reek of impending doom and regret. But that was because Davey Holmes had peed himself at the back."

Master Ra shot her a withering look over his shoulder. "Your humor is neither needed nor appreciated at this time," he said, barely containing his irritation.

Finally, the bus pulled over, stopping a block from the warehouse serving as their makeshift soup kitchen. The result was the same whether Big Tito had chosen this spot to avoid alerting anyone to their presence or because the bus was too large to navigate the narrow streets. This was where their journey with Big Tito concluded.

The bus doors opened with a pneumatic hiss, and everyone grabbed their bags, shuffling toward the exit. Master Ra's knee seemed to be acting up again, forcing everyone to wait as he painstakingly descended the steps to the sidewalk.

He led them through a labyrinth of narrow alleys that Ryu had never known existed, each turn taking them closer to the warehouse district. Their steps were soft, deliberate, almost like whispers against the gravel.

"Stay back," Master Ra warned in a hushed voice as they reached the edge of an alley with a vantage point of the warehouse. "I'll scout ahead. Wait here."

One of the boys stepped forward. "I'll go with you."

Master Ra appeared ready to object, but he nodded as if weighing some internal calculus. "If we're not back in five minutes, don't follow us."

The directive seemed meant for everyone, but his eyes found Ryu. She nodded, the gravity of the situation settling upon her like a shroud.

Indigo broke the tense silence. "Well, if we're playing hide-and-seek, I was a third-grade champion."

Master Ra shook his head, questioning his decision to let Indigo accompany them. Without another word, he disappeared around the corner with the volunteer boy.

Nerve-wracking minutes ticked by, each second stretching longer than the one before. Then, the boy returned, urgently beckoning for them to follow.

Inside, the warehouse was a disaster. It looked like a storm had ripped through, scattering debris and upending supplies. The smell of rotting food filled the air, thick and cloying. Ryu's eyes met Master Ra's; the unspoken fear was that the people who did this had also harmed their friends.

They found Master Ra in the small upstairs room where the girls had once slept, where they had hidden from their enemy. The sight of an upturned chair and a length of rope was like a punch to the gut. This was where they had tortured Marco for information.

Indigo stood beside Ryu, her gaze sweeping over the room. "Looks like someone threw a party and forgot to send us an invite."

Master Ra sighed deeply, his eyes almost pleading for patience. "Enough, Indigo. This is serious. One more, and I will chain you to a seat on the bus myself. Understood?"

"Sorry, I use humor as a defense mechanism when frightened. I'll shut up."

Ryu intervened before another word could be said, her voice urgently heavy. "We need to let people know we're back. We need to find out where they've taken Talia. And we need to do it fast."

For a moment, nobody spoke. They all knew the stakes. They all knew what had to be done. And for better or worse, they were in this together.

Ryu felt the familiar pressure of her friend Indigo's gaze as they moved about the makeshift soup kitchen. She'd been Ryu's rock, her unwavering support for so long, and that wasn't changing in a hurry. At least she was sticking to her self-imposed vow of silence. She carefully moved among the volunteers and the arriving homeless, her eyes never leaving Ryu for long. Indigo's presence had always been like a background melody to Ryu—constantly there but never intrusive. Today, however, her silence felt different, heavy with things unsaid and warnings unheeded.

The tension was palpable as they cleared the space, salvaged what could be used, and prepared for the evening. When Ryu moved to chop vegetables, she felt Indigo's eyes on her, watching every slice as though ensuring that even the knife wouldn't dare harm her friend.

Two women arrived and tut-tutted at the state of the place but also came bearing chairs. They seemed to know Master Ra and greeted him warmly but spared a scrutinizing gaze for Indigo. She met their eyes but said nothing, maintaining her silent vigil. RA shot her a withering look as if contemplating the wisdom of allowing her to come along. Indigo shrugged, her expression saying, "I'm here, aren't I?"

Soon, the first of the hungry began to appear, tentatively peering around corners, eyes widening in relief as they spotted the white tunics of Master Ra's crew. Ryu recognized one of the women she had met before and quickly ushered her to a table. When she returned to the chopping table, Indigo smiled but remained quiet.

And then Benny the Hat arrived. He was a snitch, a dangerous man to trust. Ryu smiled and waved, keeping her suspicions well hidden. When Benny disappeared as suddenly as he came, Ryu felt Indigo's eyes harden. She was piecing it together, sensing the imminent danger even if she didn't know the specifics.

Ryu walked over to Master Ra, who sat in a shadowy corner. "They'll be here before nightfall," he said, his voice laced with foreboding. "We don't want too many witnesses."

"Will he come? The leader?"

"He will. And he'll know who you are," Master Ra added ominously.

Lingering by a stack of unused bowls, Indigo looked up at that moment. Her eyes met Ryu's, and she tilted her head in a silent query. Ryu looked back at her, a mixture of reassurance and caution in her gaze. 'I'll explain later,' she tried to convey.

As the sky darkened and the atmosphere in the warehouse grew taut like a pulled bowstring, Indigo finally broke her silence. She moved next to Ryu and whispered loud enough for Master Ra to hear, "You know, silence has a weight heavier than words can carry. It's filled with all the things we don't say."

RA sighed, casting a doubtful look at Indigo. "Your friend has a poetic nature," he said to Ryu. "But I hope that weight she talks about doesn't pull us all down."

Ryu looked at Indigo, her eyes conveying more than words

ever could. Here was her friend, a guardian of sorts, fierce in her silence as she was in her words. She was not the trained warrior that Ryu was, nor did she carry the wisdom of Master Ra, but she bore the weight of her kind of strength. And in a situation where everything else was uncertain, Ryu found immense comfort in that unyielding, unspoken strength.

"As do I," Ryu responded to Master Ra. "But if anything, it will lift us. You'll see."

Indigo looked between the two, her eyes finally resting on Ryu. Her silence had been a choice, a shield, and a sword. But it was also a promise that she would be there, even if she had to carry the weight of her unsaid words like a warrior's shield.

Master Ra looked from one young woman to the other. "Very well," he said as if resigning himself to an unavoidable fate. "Let's prepare. They will be here soon, and we have much to do."

And so they did, each absorbed in their tasks but acutely aware of the others. Each fortified by their strength—Ryu's in her resolve, Master Ra's in his wisdom, and Indigo's in her weighted silence. Together, they waited for whatever darkness would come their way, a triad bound by the complexities of spoken and unspoken words.

FORTY THREE

The tension in the air had become almost tangible. Even as Ryu stood with Master Ra in the warehouse shadows, she could feel the nerves running through the assembled members of their group. Everyone was waiting, their eyes flicking between the darkening horizon and the old warehouse clock, its hands ticking away the seconds like water droplets falling from a leaky tap.

The moment they had all been waiting for arrived with the ominous rumble of engines in the distance. Four black cars pulled up in front of the warehouse. The men who emerged were an intimidating spectacle, each one exuding a sense of menace that seemed to stretch the growing darkness around them. They were soldiers of uncertainty, harbingers of dread, and had come for one purpose.

Master Ra's grip tightened on Ryu's arm to anchor her to the shadows. "Stay here," he whispered, the words barely audible but drenched in gravity that made Ryu feel as though the fate of their world hinged on her obedience.

Behind them, lurking in the shadows, Indigo. As she felt the tension ratcheting up, she was second-guessing her insistence. What could she do? She tightened her lips, biting down on the urge to make a wry comment. She focused on being as invisible as she could.

Finally, the rear door of the last car swung open. Another man stepped out, and Ryu strained her eyes; sure, she caught a fleeting glimpse of another figure and heard a murmur—a voice, her name—before the door was slammed shut.

Talia. It had to be Talia.

"Where is she?" The man's voice cracked like a whip through the silence, every syllable tinged with impatience and malice.

Master Ra whispered again, his grip still firm on Ryu's arm. "Stay here." Then he stepped away, moving toward the light, a moth attracted to the flame that could consume him.

He emerged into the halo of the floodlight. "Let the girl go," RA's voice was a contrast, soft yet powerful, each word deliberate and filled with underlying meaning. Ryu noticed how he limped slightly, betraying his knee injury. She clenched her fists, desperately wanting to run to his aid, but remembering his directive, she remained anchored.

The man laughed, a cold laugh that sent chills down Indigo's spine. "RA! Hiding, were we? Too scared to face reality?"

"I'm here now," RA countered, unflinching. "Let the girl go. She isn't the one you seek."

In the back, Indigo could feel her own heart pounding as if it wanted to escape. She glanced at Ryu and saw her anxiety mirrored. And it was amplified. Her fingers itched to intervene, to make some sarcastic comment that would deflate the gravity of the situation, but she restrained herself. A wry comment would earn more than withering looks from Master Ra. Silence was a virtue.

"Safe," RA finally said, as if weighing each letter of the word. "Now, if you have an issue with me, let's settle this man-to-man."

The man's laugh, louder this time, was devoid of genuine amusement. "You're all show, RA, no substance."

"Then prove it," RA shot back. "Let the girl go. She means nothing to you."

"She's my daughter!"

The words seemed to hang in the air, a sudden fog of confusion clouding Ryu's mind. She felt a hand clutch her arm—Indigo, her face as flushed as Ryu felt. Daughter? Could he be the man they had been told was dead? A father leading the hunt for his daughter?

"No, she isn't; as you know, you took the wrong girl. You snatched up Ryu's foster sister. There is no bond of blood, and you have no hold over Ryu; you gave that up a long time ago," RA declared, his voice edged with disdain.

The man smirked. "Perhaps, but blood is blood."

"Let Talia go," RA stated, his eyes narrowing. "She isn't your child. She is an innocent here."

The man's laugh was a sound Ryu would never forget. "You know more than I thought," he conceded, locking eyes with RA as if acknowledging a worthy opponent. She didn't remember his face. Could she honestly have forgotten the face of her father?

All the while, Indigo had edged closer, her heart in her throat. She was now near enough to see the faces clearly, close enough to be part of the unfolding drama but still far enough to remain unseen. She felt caught in a web of conflicting emotions—fear, concern, regret, and most of all, the gnawing sensation that the night was far from over. Indigo met Ryu's eyes for just a moment. Both knew, without words, that whatever happened next would change them forever.

The tension in the air was palpable, an electrical charge that tightened the skin and made the hairs stand on end. Ryu's eyes flickered across the men before her, settling on her father, who exuded an unhinged, malevolent satisfaction.

Master Ra, standing across from him, was calm amidst the storm, but Ryu could sense an undercurrent of unease. His face was etched with lines that seemed to deepen as the confrontation unfolded, and Ryu could see him favoring his injured knee, subtle but evident to those who knew him well.

As RA made his deliberate advance, Ryu's attention was torn by a flicker of movement in the periphery. A shadow detached itself from the deeper darkness, moving almost fluidly—Indigo. She was there but not there, a whisper in the wind, a shadow within shadows.

"Where is the girl? Where is my *real* daughter?" Ryu's father snarled, interrupting her thoughts.

Master Ra didn't falter but continued his slow, almost unbearable progress toward Ryu's father. He reached him, and for a moment, time seemed to slow, each heartbeat a loud drum in Ryu's ears. A sudden, swift motion split the silence—RA lashing out, a serpent strike aimed to incapacitate. Ryu's father dodged and counterattacked. The dance was on.

For all RA's wisdom and skill, his body betrayed him. Ryu's father launched a vicious kick at his knee, and RA fell, a grimace of pain flashing across his face.

"I'm here!" Ryu's voice shattered the tension, charging into the open. "Now leave him alone and let my sister go. It's me you want!"

Her father's twisted smile widened as he stepped toward her.

"Ryu, my daughter, The Last of the Dragons. You are a sight for sore eyes after all these years."

As he said this, from the corner of her eye, Ryu noticed Indigo moving—swift and low, circling to the other side of the makeshift battleground. She was aiming for the car where Talia was held captive.

"I said, let my sister go!" Ryu yelled, pulling attention back to herself.

Her father nodded to one of his men, who moved to the car to release Talia. Indigo struck as the car door opened, disabling the man with a swift, almost invisible movement.

"Run, Ryu!" Talia screamed as she stumbled out, her eyes meeting Indigo's momentarily, a silent thank you. "He's going to kill you!"

"I know," Ryu's voice was cold steel. "But if he's going to do that, he'll have to beat me first. And that won't be easy. Believe me. I'm not the little girl he left thinking he was dead."

Her father laughed maniacally, not noticing—or perhaps ignoring—that Indigo had now slipped back into the shadows, her presence a mystery. "If that's how you want it, I'll try to be gentle with you. Shall we do it here and now?"

"No time like the present," Ryu responded, her eyes never leaving her father's face. But in her peripheral vision, she noted Indigo's shadow merging with the others. Ryu felt a newfound resolve, strengthened by Indigo's invisible support and her sister's freedom.

It was then that Ryu realized something crucial: the shriveled piece of flesh, the source of her father's deranged confidence, was no longer strapped to his hand. Whether he'd lost it in the scuffle or had grown too arrogant to think he'd need it, Ryu didn't know. But it was the opening she had been waiting for.

The tension, drawn taut as a bowstring, finally snapped. And in that moment, every player in this macabre drama knew that the endgame had begun.

FORTY FOUR

As the tension thickened like the clouds of an impending storm, Ryu sensed the unmistakable aura of Indigo lurking in the background, striving to be both unseen and unheard. Indigo had never been a fan of confrontations, but this was family; this was important. And it was liable to get her killed. She blended into the shadows like a specter, her eyes narrowing at the unfolding drama.

Master Ra's ruse hadn't escaped Ryu, a realization that slightly tilted the scales of this hazardous gambit, but how slight?

When her father's eyes flickered with the dawning awareness of the trick, it was as if electricity coursed through the air, a jolt of raw tension. "Stop that girl and bring her back here!" His words came out as a venomous snarl, dripping with the promise of retribution. "I will deal with you later, RA."

That girl.

Indigo.

Ryu felt her father's anger gnawing at the edges of the scene like a feral beast; it was a frantic, palpable thing. She felt no connection to him; at that moment, she couldn't reconcile him with the man she had idolized as a kid. She sized up the men near the cars—goons by appearance and likely armed. None moved. They were statues, paralyzed in the theater of their boss's wrath. "It would be easier if you just came with me, Ryu. I'm not going to hurt you, I promise," he said, sounding almost sincere. "You're my little Ru-Ru. We are family, kiddo. This is in our blood. Embrace it."

As if sugared words could ever sway her. "And become what? A caged bird waiting for whatever sinister plans you've dreamed up? No thanks."

At that moment, his eyes flashed with malevolence, the mask dropping, but Ryu was weary of words.

She'd lived her entire life trusting no one outside of her circle of Indigo and Thalia, and that wasn't about to change just because he'd come back from the dead.

She advanced, her movement a blend of grace and urgency, a dancer with deadly intentions. She feinted, tricking him into grasping at empty air, making him appear the fool. The embarrassment mutated into fury within seconds. Seizing the moment, Ryu's foot rocketed upwards, the impact against his ribs satisfyingly solid.

As Ryu and her father stood locked in their silent battle of wills, a profound transformation began to take place within her. The latent dragon energy that coursed through her veins began to awaken, surging like a fiery tide. With a sudden eruption of power, Ryu's body was enveloped in a shimmering aura of fire, a supernatural phenomenon that bathed her in a blazing, ethereal light. Her eyes blazed with intensity, and she felt a newfound strength coursing through her limbs. In this moment of transformation, Ryu was no longer bound by the limitations of mere mortals. She could jump higher, run faster, and move with a grace and agility that defied the laws of physics. The air around her crackled with the energy of a dragon, and she was ready to unleash its might. Her father, too, seemed to tap into superhuman skills. His movements became lightning-fast, his strikes precise, and his reflexes uncanny. It was a battle of epic proportions, a clash of titans.

Ryu advanced with newfound confidence, her every move a mesmerizing dance of fire and fury. Her father, no longer weighed down by his previous injuries, met her with equal ferocity. Their blows were like thunderclaps, each strike resonating with the power of dragons. They circled each other with the grace of martial artists, their movements a blur of speed and precision. Ryu's fire aura flickered and danced around her, leaving a trail of fiery sparks in its wake. As the battle raged on, it became clear that this was no ordinary confrontation. It was a battle of elemental forces, of ancient power awakened. The very ground seemed to tremble beneath their feet as they clashed. Ryu's dragon energy allowed her to anticipate her father's moves accurately. She weaved between his strikes, delivering devastating blows of her own. With every punch and kick, the fiery aura around her intensified, leaving scorch marks on the earth. Her father, too, was a force to be reckoned with. He moved with a whirlwind speed, countering Ryu's attacks with lightning-fast reflexes. It was a spectacle of martial prowess and supernatural power, a battle that defied explanation. As they continued to trade blows, Ryu felt the dragon energy within her surging to its peak. With a mighty roar, she unleashed a torrent of fire from her very being, engulfing her father in a searing inferno. He cried out in agony as the flames consumed him, and for a moment, it seemed as though he might be defeated. But her father, fueled by his supernatural abilities, fought back. He emerged from the flames, his body unscathed, and launched a final, desperate attack.

Ryu met him head-on, their clash creating shockwaves that rippled through the air. In the end, Ryu's unwavering determination and the power of her dragon energy prevailed. With a final, devastating strike, she sent her father hurtling backward, his body crashing to the ground in defeat. The battle had taken its toll on both of them, but Ryu stood victorious, her dragon aura still blazing brightly. The white-clothed disciples of Master Ra approached cautiously, their respect evident in their eyes.

Ryu's transformation had been miraculous, a testament to the ancient power that flowed through her veins. As she caught her breath, she knew this was only the beginning of her journey, a path paved with fire and destiny. The finality of the battle hung in the air like the echo of a dirge, merging with the gunpowder and the sweat, the fear and the triumph. But this conclusion brought no relief, no celebration, just a heavy sense of closure. Ryu took a deep, shuddering breath as Indigo emerged from her hidden position, her eyes wide with awe and horror. Ryu had battled her demons and emerged victorious, but the cost of this victory remained uncertain. One thing, however, was painfully clear: There was no turning back. The flames of destiny had been ignited, and Ryu was now a force to be reckoned with, a true master of the Dragon's power.

FORTY FIVE

It was over. The weight of that realization washed over Ryu like a flood, sweeping away the immediate dangers and fears. Her lungs filled with air that no longer tasted of impending doom.

Master Ra had recovered the mysterious hand from Indigo, who had ferreted it away from the warehouse, taking a mad risk with her own life in that one stupid, heroic moment. Ryu's father's menacing but leaderless minions were all restrained, waiting for their uncertain fates to be determined. But it wasn't just their incapacitation that brought Ryu relief; it was the inexplicable, astonishing transformation of her father's body. It burst into flames like heaven and earth conspired to erase his evil essence. His self-combustion was an enigma, a perplexing finale to a chapter of her life she had never wanted to read. The concrete where he'd lain was now a charred monument to his ignominious end.

And then there was that shadow, the elusive figure she had caught a glimpse of in the car window. What was it? Some spirit? Some lingering vestige of her newfound strength? These thoughts spun in her head, but for now, they were secondary. They could wait. Survival, for the moment, was enough.

Master Ra limped toward her, his usual stern demeanor softened by the extraordinary events. "He called me the Last Dragon," Ryu said, almost whispering as if saying it louder would summon another calamity.

"And so you are," Master Ra said firmly. "You carry the essence of that ancient entity, the energy that has persisted since the time of the pharaoh."

"The demon?" Ryu asked cautiously, still grappling with her internal labyrinth of questions and revelations.

"No, not the demon. The spirit that kept the demon at bay. That, I believe, aided you against me and your father," he explained.

The comfort in knowing this was fleeting. "At least that's over," Ryu mused aloud.

Master Ra raised an eyebrow. "Don't be so sure. Flames didn't defeat that demon. It simply relinquished its host. It will likely seek another."

Across the makeshift battleground, Ryu noticed Indigo, no longer lurking in the margins but comforting Talia. The younger girl looked fragile, a stark contrast to her usual bravado. Indigo's eyes met Ryu's, and in that brief connection, both shared the weight of what had happened and, perhaps, what was yet to come.

"So, what's next for the demon?" Ryu asked, redirecting her attention to Master Ra.

"Uncertain," he shrugged. "But the spirit within you, your Dragon, is both a governor and a catalyst for that demon. They'll likely cross paths again, each vying for control, for completion."

Ryu's eyes narrowed. "So, you'll safeguard the hand?"

"No, I'll see it destroyed. That relic is too dangerous to exist," he asserted, wiping away the last vestige of Ryu's lingering doubts. "The hand could've united the spirit and demon in a calamitous fusion. It's best gone."

Ryu took a deep breath. She looked again at the burnt patch where her father had met his end. "Did that spirit change him?" she wondered aloud. "Or was he always like that? Did I ever really know him? My father…" she shook her head. "No. He wasn't my father. Jack was more of a father to me than that man ever was."

"As you say, all I can tell you is that there was darkness in him long before the spirit," Master Ra added.

She felt a chill. "There was a homeless woman. She claimed she knew him, said he had the touch of the Dragon."

"Maybe he did. Through the lineage, perhaps. Through your mother. That was the bloodline, never through the male side."

As they spoke, Ryu watched Indigo consoling Talia, two souls bound by a shared experience, an unspoken understanding of the battle fought and the war ahead. The tangible connection snapped Ryu back to the present.

"What now?" Ryu questioned, gesturing at the remains of their surroundings.

"We rebuild," Master Ra said, his eyes sweeping across the faces of those who remained. "I won't return to the temple just yet. There's work to be done here."

"And them?" Ryu nodded toward her father's apprehended men.

"A friend in the police will sort them out," he explained. "For us, they're inconsequential now."

"And you? Will you stay?" he asked.

"Here? Yes," she said, her eyes drifting toward Indigo and Talia again. "For now, at least. We must get Indigo back to her family and ensure she's safe."

"Very well," Master Ra said, looking profoundly at Ryu. "You've come into your inheritance, Dragon. And we both know your journey is far from over."

Ryu nodded again on the scorched earth where her father

had lain. Uncertainty still fogged the horizon, but she felt an unparalleled relief for now. Today, she had looked into the abyss and had not blinked. Whatever else the future held, she knew she could face it.

Master Ra turned to leave, but Ryu lingered for a moment longer, absorbing the surreality of it all. Amidst the chaos, the danger, and the inexplicable, there was a serenity in survival, a quiet triumph in enduring. And for now, that was more than enough.

As she walked away, her thoughts shifted to the immediate tasks—rebuilding, reuniting Indigo with her family, and perhaps, understanding the extraordinary spirit that had chosen her as its host. But for the moment, Ryu reveled in survival's simple yet profound sweetness. The Dragon within her lay dormant but vigilant, ready for whatever came next.

THE END

Thank you for exploring the tale of "The Dragon." If Ryu's story of resilience and discovery resonated with you, consider sharing your thoughts with a review on Amazon or Goodreads. Your feedback is invaluable, not just to us, but to fellow readers navigating their next literary adventure. Please ensure your review complies with the platform's Community Guidelines.

For more information or to discover similar stories, visit us at www.kingstonimperial.com or contact info@kingstonimperial.com.